SWORDS OF THE RED
BROTHERHOOD

BY

ROBERT E. HOWARD

British Library Cataloguing-in-Publication Data
A catalogue record for this book is available from the
British Library

Contents

Robert E. Howard

Robert Ervin Howard was born in Peaster, Texas in 1906. During his youth, his family moved between a variety of Texan boomtowns, and Howard – a bookish and somewhat introverted child – was steeped in the violent myths and legends of the Old South. Although he loved reading and learning, Howard developed a distinctly Texan, hardboiled outlook on the world. He became a passionate fan of boxing, taking it up at an amateur level, and from the age of nine began to write adventure tales of semi-historical bloodshed. In 1919, when Howard was thirteen, his family moved to the Central Texas hamlet of Cross Plains, where he would stay for the rest of his life.

At fifteen Howard began to read the pulp magazines of the day, and to write more seriously. The December 1922 issue of his high school newspaper featured two of his stories, 'Golden Hope Christmas' and 'West is West'. In 1924 he sold his first piece – a short caveman tale titled 'Spear and Fang' – for $16 to the not-yet-famous *Weird Tales* magazine. He published with the magazine regularly over the next few years. 1929 was a breakout year for Howard, in that the 23-year-old writer began to sell to other magazines, such as *Ghost Stories* and *Argosy*, both of whom had previously sent him hundreds of rejection slips. In 1930, he began a correspondence with weird fiction master H. P. Lovecraft which ran up to his death six years later, and is regarded as one of the great correspondence cycles in all of fantasy literature.

It was partly due to Lovecraft's encouragement that Howard created his most famous character, Conan the Cimmerian. Conan – a barbarian-turned-King during the Hyborian Age, a mythical period of some 12,000 years ago – featured in seventeen *Weird Tales* stories between 1933 and 1936, and is now regarded as having spawned the 'sword and sorcery' genre, making Howard's influence on fantasy literature comparable to that of J. R. R. Tolkien's. The Conan stories have since been adapted many times, most famously in the series of films starring Arnold Schwarzenegger.

Howard was enjoying an all-time high in sales by the beginning of 1936, but he was also deeply upset by the ill health of his mother, who had fallen into a coma. On the morning of June 11, 1936, he asked an attending nurse whether she would ever recover, and the nurse replied negatively. Howard walked to his car, parked outside the family home in Cross Plains, and shot himself. He died eight hours later, aged just thirty.

CHAPTER 1

One moment the glade lay empty; the next a man poised tensely at the edge of the bushes. No sound warned the red squirrels of his coming, but the birds that flitted about in the sunlight took sudden fright at the apparition and rose in a clamoring swarm. The man scowled and glanced quickly back the way he had come, fearing the bird-flight might have betrayed his presence. Then he started across the glade, placing his feet with caution. Tall and muscular of frame, he moved with the supple ease of a panther.

He was naked except for a rag twisted about his loins, and his limbs were criss-crossed with scratches from briars and caked with dried mud. A brown-crusted bandage was knotted about his thickly muscled left arm. Under a matted, black mane, his face was drawn and gaunt, and his eyes burned like the eyes of a wounded animal. He limped slightly as he picked his way along the dim path that crossed the open space.

Half-way across the glade, the man stopped short and wheeled about, as a long-drawn call quavered from the forest behind. It sounded much like the howl of a wolf. But he knew it was no wolf.

Rage burned in his bloodshot eyes as he turned once more and sped along the path which, as it left the glade, ran along the edge of a dense thicket that rose in a solid clump of greenery among the trees and bushes. His glance caught and was held by a massive log, deeply embedded in the grassy earth. It lay parallel to the fringe of the thicket. He halted again, and looked back across the glade. To the untutored eye, there were no signs to show that he had passed, but to his wilderness-trained sight, the traces of his passage were quite evident. And he knew that his pursuers could read his tracks without effort. He snarled silently, the red rage growing in his eyes, the berserk fury of a hunted beast which is ready to turn at bay, and drew war-axe and hunting knife from the girdle which upheld his loinclout.

Then he walked swiftly down the trail with deliberate carelessness, here and there crushing a grass-blade beneath his foot. However when he had reached the further end of the great log, he sprang upon it, turned and ran lightly along its back. The bark had long been worn away by the elements. Now he left no sign to alert those behind him that he had doubled on his trail. As he reached the densest point of the thicket, he faded into it like a shadow, with scarcely the quiver of' a leaf to mark his passing.

The minutes dragged. The red squirrels chattered again on the branches . . . then flattened their bodies and were suddenly mute. Again the glade was invaded. As silently as the first man had appeared, three other men emerged from the eastern edge of the clearing. They were dark-skinned men, naked but for beaded buckskin loin-cloths and moccasins, and they were hideously painted.

They had scanned the glade carefully before moving into the open. Then they slipped out of the bushes without hesitation, in close single-file, treading softly and bending down to stare at the path. Even for these human bloodhounds, following the trail of the white man was no easy task. As they moved slowly across the glade, one man stiffened, grunted, and pointed with a flint-tipped spear at a crushed grass-blade where the path entered the forest again. All halted instantly, their beady black eyes searching the forest walls. But their quarry was well hidden. They detected nothing to indicate that he was crouched within a few yards of them. Presently, they moved on again, more rapidly now, following the faint marks that seemed to betray that their prey had grown careless through weakness or desperation.

Just as they passed the spot where the thicket crowded closest to the ancient trail, the white man bounded into the path behind them and plunged his knife between the shoulders of the last man. The attack was so swift and unexpected, the Indian had no chance to save himself. The blade was in his heart before he knew he was in peril. The other two whirled with the instant, steel-trap quickness of savages, but even as his knife sank home, the white man struck a tremendous blow with the war-axe in his right hand.

The second Indian caught the blow just as he was turning, and it split his skull.

The remaining Indian rushed savagely to the attack. He stabbed at the white man's breast even as the killer wrenched his axe from the dead man's skull. With amazing dexterity, the white man hurled the limp body against the savage, then followed it with an attack as furious and desperate as the lunge of a wounded tiger. The Indian, staggering under the impact of the corpse, made no attempt to parry the dripping axe. The instinct to slay submerging even the instinct to live, he drove his spear ferociously at his enemy's broad breast. But the white man had the advantage of a quicker mind, and a weapon in each hand. His axe struck the spearaside, and the knife in the brawny left hand ripped upward into the painted belly.

A frightful howl burst from the Indian's lips as he crumpled, disembowelled-a cry not of fear or pain, but of baffled bestial fury, the death screech of a panther. It was answered by a while chorus of yells some distance east of the glade. The white man started convulsively, wheeled, crouching like a wild thing at bay, lips asnarl. Blood trickled down his forearm from under the bandage.

With an incoherent imprecation, he turned and fled westward. He did not pick his way now, but ran with all the speed of his long legs. Behind him for a space, the woods were silent, than a demoniacal howling burst from the spot he had just quitted. His pursuers had found the bodies of his victims. He had no breath for cut-sing and the blood from his freshly-opened wound left a trail a child could follow. He had hoped that the three Indians he had slain were all of the war-party that still pursued him. But he might have known these human wolves never quit a blood trail.

The woods were silent again, and that meant they were racing after him, his path betrayed by the trail of blood he could not check.

A wind out of the west blew against his face, laden with salty dampness. He registered a vague surprise. If he was that close to the sea, then the long chase had been even longer than he had realized. But it was nearly over. Even his wolfish vitality was ebbing under the terrific strain. He gasped for breath and there was a sharp pain in his side. His legs trembled with weariness and the lame one ached like a knife-cut in the tendons each time he set the foot to the earth. Fiercely he had followed the instincts of the wilderness which bred him, straining every nerve and sinew, exhausting every subtlety and artifice to survive. Now in his extremity, he was obeying another instinct, seeking a place to turn at bay and sell his life at a bloody price.

He did not leave the trail for the tangled depths on either hand. Now he knew it was futile to hope to evade his pursuers. On he ran down the trail, while the blood pounded louder and louder in his ears and each breath he drew was a racking, dry-lipped gulp. Behind him a mad baying broke out, token that they were close on his heels and expecting to overhaul him soon. They would come as fleet as starving wolves now, howling at every leap.

Abruptly he burst from the denseness of the trees and saw ahead of him the ground pitching upward, and the ancient trail winding up rocky ledges between jagged boulders. A dizzy red mist swam before him, as he scanned the hill he had come to, a rugged crag rising sheer from the forest about its foot. And the dim trail wound up to a broad ledge near the summit.

That ledge would be as good a place as any to die. He limped up the trail, going on hands and knees in the steeper places, his knife between his teeth. He had not yet reached the jutting ledge when some forty painted savages broke from among the trees.

Their screams rose to a devil's crescendo as they raced toward the foot of the crag, loosing arrows as they came. The shafts showered about the man who doggedly climbed upward, and one stuck in the calf of his leg. Without pausing in his climb, he tore it out and threw it aside, heedless of the less accurate missiles which splintered on the rocks about him. Grimly he hauled himself over the rim of the ledge, and turned about, drawing his hatchet and shifting knife to hand. He lay glaring down at his pursuers over the rim, only his shock of hair and his blazing eyes visible. His great chest heaved as he drank in the air in huge, shuddering gasps, and he clenched his teeth against an uneasy nausea.

The warriors came on, leaping agilely over the rocks at the foot of the hill, some changing bows for war-axes. The first to reach the crag was a brawny chief with an eagle-feather in his braided hair. He halted briefly, one foot on the sloping trail, arrow notched and drawn half-way back, head thrown back and lips parted for a yell. But the shaft was never loosed. He froze into statuesque immobility, and the blood-lust in his black eyes gave way to a glare of startled recognition. With a whoop he recoiled, throwing his arms wide to check the rush of his howling braves. The man crouching on the ledge above them understood their tongue, but he was too high above them to catch the significance of the staccato phrases snapped at the warriors by the eagle-feathered chief.

But all ceased their yelping and stood mutely staring up-not at the man on the ledge, but at the hill itself. Then without further hesitation, they unstrung their bows and thrust them into buckskin cases beside their quivers; turned their backs and trotted across the open space, to melt into the forest without a backward look.

The white man glared after them in amazement, recognizing the finality expressed in the departure. He knew they would not come back. They were heading for their village, a hundred miles to the east.

But it was inexplicable. What was there about his refuge that would cause a red war-party to abandon a chase it had followed so long with all the passion of hungry wolves'? There was a red score between him and them. He had been their prisoner, and he had escaped, and in that escape a famous war-chief had died. That was why the braves had followed him so relentlessly, over broad rivers and mountains and through long leagues of gloomy forest, the hunting grounds of hostile tribes. And now the survivors of that long chase turned back when their enemy was run to earth and trapped. He shook his head, abandoning the riddle.

He rose gingerly, dizzy from the long grind, and scarcely able to realize that it was over. His limbs were stiff, his wounds ached. He spat dryly and cursed, rubbing his burning, bloodshot eyes with the back of his thick wrist. He blinked and took stock of his surroundings. Below him the green wilderness waved and billowed away and away in a solid mass, and above its western rim rose a steel-blue haze he knew hung over the ocean. The wind stirred his black mane, and the salt tang of the atmosphere revived him. He expanded his enormous chest and drank it in.

Then he turned stiffly and painfully about, growling at the twinge in his bleeding calf, and investigated the ledge whereon he stood. Behind it rose a sheer, rocky cliff to the crest of the crag, some thirty feet above him. A narrow ladder-like stair of hand-holds had been niched into the rock. And a few feet away, there was a cleft in the wall, wide enough and tall enough to admit a man.

He limped to the cleft, peered in, and grunted explosively. The sun, hanging high above the western forest, slanted into the cleft, revealing a tunnel-like cavern beyond, and faintly illumined the arch at which this tunnel ended. In that arch was set a heavy iron-bound door!

His eyes narrowed, unbelieving. This country was a howling wilderness. For a thousand miles this coast ran bare and uninhabited except for the squalid villages of fish-eating tribes, who were even lower in the scale of life than their forest-dwelling brothers. He had never questioned his notion that he was probably the first man of his color ever to set foot in this area. Yet there stood that mysterious door, mute evidence of European civilization.

Being inexplicable, it was an object of suspicion, and suspiciously he approached it, axe and knife ready. Then as his blood-shot eyes became more accustomed to the soft gloom that lurked on either side of the narrow shaft of sunlight, he noticed something else-thick, iron-bound chests ranged along the walls. A blaze of comprehension came into his eyes. He bent over one, but the lid resisted his efforts. Lifting his hatchet to shatter the ancient lock, he abruptly changed his mind and limped toward the arched door. His bearing was more confident now, his weapons hung at his sides. He pushed against the ornately-carved door and it swung inward without resistance.

Then his manner changed again. With lightning-like speed, he recoiled with a startled curse, knife and hatchet flashing to positions of defense. He poised there like a statue of menace, craning his massive neck to glare through the door. It was darker in the large natural chamber into which he was looking, but a dim glow emanated from a shining heap in the center of the great ebony table about which sat those silent shapes whose appearance had so startled him.

They did not move; they did not turn their heads.

"Are you all drunk?" he demanded harshly.

There was no reply. He was not a man easily abashed, yet now he was disconcerted.

"You might offer me a glass of that wine you're swigging," he growled. "By Satan, you show poor courtesy to a man who's been one of your own brotherhood. Are you going to. . ." H is voice trailed off into silence, and in silence he stood and stared awhile at those fantastic figures sitting so silently and still about the great ebon table.

"They're not drunk," he muttered presently. "They're not even drinking. What devil's game is this?"

He stepped across the threshold and was instantly fighting for his life against the murderous, unseen fingers that clutched so suddenly at his throat.

CHAPTER 2

And on the beach, not many miles from the cavern where the silent figures sat, other, denser shadows were gathering over the tangled lives of men ....

Francoise d'Chastillon idly stirred a sea-shell with a daintily slippered toe, comparing its delicate pink edges to the first pink haze of dawn that rose over the misty beaches. It was not dawn now, but the sun was not long up, and the pearl-grey mist which drifted over the waters had not yet been dispelled.

Francoise lifted her splendidly shaped head and stared out over a scene alien and repellent to her, yet drearily familiar in every detail. From her feet the tawny sands ran to meet the softly lapping waves which stretched westward to be lost in the blue haze of the horizon. She was standing on the southern curve of the bay, and south of her the land sloped upward to the low ridge which formed one horn of that bay. From that ridge, she knew, one could look southward across the bare waters-into infinities of distance as absolute as the view to west and north.

Turning landward, she absently scanned the fortress which had been her home for the past year. Against the cerulean sky floated the golden and scarlet banner of her house. She made out the figures of men toiling in the gardens and fields that huddled near the fort, which, itself, seemed to shrink from the gloomy rampart of the forest fringing the open belt on the east, and stretching north and south as far as she could see. Beyond it, to the east, loomed a great mountain range that shut off the coast from the continent that lay behind it. Francoise feared that mountain-flanked forest, and her fear was shared by every one in the tiny settlement. Death lurked in those whispering depths, death swift and terrible, death slow and hideous, hidden, painted, tireless.

She sighed and moved listlessly toward the water's edge. The dragging days were all one color, and the world of cities and courts and gaiety seemed not only thousands of miles, but long ages away. Again she sought in vain for the reason that had caused a Count of France to flee with his retainers to this wild coast, exchanging the castle of his ancestors for a hut of logs.

Her eyes softened at the light patter of small bare feet across the sands. A young girl quite naked, came running over the low sandy ridge, her slight body dripping, and her flaxen hair plastered wetly on her small head. Her wistful eyes were wide with excitement.

"Oh, my Lady!" she cried. "My Lady!"

Breathless from her scamper, she made incoherent gestures. Francoise smiled and put an arm about the child. In her lonely life Francoise bestowed the tenderness of a naturally affectionate nature on the pitiful waif she had picked up in the French port from which the long voyage had begun.

"What are you trying to tell me, Tina? Get your breath, child."

"A ship!" cried the girl, pointing southward. "I was swimming in a pool the sea had hollowed in the sand on the other side of the ridge, and I saw it! A ship sailing up out of the south!"

She tugged at Francoise's hand, her slender body all aquiver. And Francoise felt her own heart beat faster at the thought of an unknown visitor. They had seen no sail since coming to that barren shore.

Tina flitted ahead of her over the yellow sands. They mounted the low, undulating ridge, and Tina poised there, a slender white figure against the clearing sky, her wet hair blowing about her thin face, a frail arm outstretched.

"Look, my Lady!"

Francoise had already seen it---a white sail, filled with the freshening wind, beating up along the coast, a few miles from the point. Her heart skipped a beat. A small event can loom large in colorless and isolated lives; but Francoise felt a premonition of evil. She felt that this sail was not here by mere chance. The nearest port was Panama, thousands of miles to the south. What brought this stranger to lonely d'Chastillon Bay?

Tina pressed close to her mistress, apprehension pinching her thin features.

"Who can it be, my Lady?" she stammered, the wind whipping color into her pale cheeks. "Is it the man the Count fears?"

Francoise looked down at her, her brow shadowed.

"Why do you say that, child? [low do you know my uncle fears anyone?"

"He must," returned Tina naively, "or he would never have come to hide in this lonely spot. Look, my Lady, how fast it comes!"

"We must go and inform my uncle," murmured Francoise. "Get your clothes, Tina. Hurry!"

The child scampered down the low slope to the pool where she had been bathing when she sighted the craft, and snatched up the slippers, stockings and dress she had left lying on the sand. She skipped back up the ridge, hopping grotesquely as she donned them in mid-flight.

Francoise, anxiously watching the approaching sail, caught her hand and they hurried toward the fort.

A few moments after they had entered the gate of the log stockade which enclosed the building, the strident blare of a bugle startled both the workers in the gardens and the men just opening the boat-house doors to push the fishing boats down their rollers to the water's edge.

Every man outside the fort dropped whatever he was doing and ran for the stockade, and every head was twisted over its shoulder to gaze fearfully at the dark line of woodland to the east. Not one looked seaward.

They thronged through the gate, shouting questions at the sentries who patrolled the firing-ledges built below the points of the upright logs.

"What is it? Why are we called in? Are the Indians coming'?"

For answer one taciturn man-at-arms pointed southward. From his vantage point the sail was now visible. Men climbed on the ledge, staring toward the sea.

On a small lookout tower on the roof of the fort, Count Henri d'Chastillon watched the onsweeping sail as it rounded the point of the southern horn. The Count was a lean man of late middle age. He was dark, somber of countenance. His trunk-hose and doublet were of black silk; the only color about his costume were the jewels that twinkled on his sword hilt, and the wine-colored cloak thrown carelessly over his shoulder. He twisted his thin black mustache nervously and turned gloomy eyes on his major-domo-a leather featured man in steel and satin.

"What do you make of it, Gallot?"

"I have seen that ship before," answered the majordomo. "Nay, I think-look there!"

A chorus of cries below them echoed his ejaculation; the ship had cleared the point and was slanting inward across the bay. And all saw the flag that suddenly broke forth from the masthead-a black flag, with white skull and crossbones gleaming in the sun.

"A cursed pirate!" exclaimed Gallot. "Aye, I know that craft! It is Harston's War-Hawk. What is he doing on this naked coast?"

"He means us no good," growled the Count. The massive gates had been closed and the captain of his men-at-arms, gleaming in steel, was directing his men to their stations, some to the firing-ledge, others to the lower loop-holes. He was massing his main strength along the western wall, in the middle of which was the gate.

A hundred men shared Count Henri's exile, both soldiers and retainers. There were forty soldiers, veteran mercenaries, wearing armor and skilled in the use of sword and arquebus. The others, house-servants and laborers, wore shirts of toughened leather, and were armed mostly with hunting bows, woodsmen's axes and boar-spears. Brawny stalwarts, they took their places scowling at the oncoming vessel, as it swung inshore, its brass work flashing in the sun. They could see steel twinkling along the rail, and hear the shouts of the seamen.

The Count had left the tower, and having donned helmet and cuirass, he betook himself to the palisade. The women of the retainers stood silently in the doorways of their huts, built inside the stockade, and quieted the clamor of their children. Francoise and Tina watched eagerly from an upper window in the fort, and Francoise felt the child's tense little body all aquiver within the crook of her protecting arm.

"They will cast anchor near the boat-house," murmured Francoise. "Yes! There goes their anchor, a hundred yards offshore. Do not tremble so, child! They can not take the fort. Perhaps they wish only fresh water and meat."

"They are coming ashore in long boats!" exclaimed the child. "Oh, my Lady, I am afraid! How the sun strikes fire from their pikes and cutlasses! Will they eat us?"

In spite of her apprehension, Francoise burst into laughter.

"Of course not! Who put that idea into your head?"

"Jacques Piriou told me the English eat women."

"He was teasing you. The English are cruel, but they are no worse than the Frenchmen who call themselves buccaneers. Piriou was one of them."

"He was cruel," muttered the child. "I'm glad the Indians cut his head off."

"Hush, child." Francoise shuddered. "Look, they have reached the shore. They line the beach and one of them is coming toward the fort. That must be Harston."

"Ahoy, the fort there!" came a hail in a voice as gusty as the wind. "I come under a flag of truce!"

19

The Count's helmeted head appeared over the points of the palisade and surveyed the pirate somberly. Harston had halted just within good ear-shot. He was a big man, bareheaded, his tawny hair blowing in the wind.

"Speak!" commanded Henri. "I have few words for men of your breed!"

Harston laughed with his lips, not with his eyes.

"I never thought to meet you on this naked coast, d'Chastillon," said he. "By Satan, I got the start of my life a little while ago when I saw your scarlet falcon floating over a fortress where I'd thought to see only bare beach. You've found it, of course?"

"Found what?" snapped the Count impatiently.

"Don't try to dissemble with me?" The pirate's stormy nature showed itself momentarily. "I know why you came here; I've come for the same reason. Where's your ship?"

"That's none of your affair, sirrah."

"You have none," confidently asserted the pirate. "I see pieces of a galleon's masts in that stockade. Your ship was wrecked! Otherwise you'd sailed away with your plunder long ago."

"What are you talking about, damn you'?" yelled the Count. "Am I a pirate to burn and plunder? Even so, what would I loot on this bare coast?"

"That which you came to find," answered the pirate coolly. "The same thing I'm after. I'm easy to deal with-

20

just give me the loot and I'll go my way and leave you in peace."

"You must be mad," snarled Henri. "I came here to find solitude and seclusion, which I enjoyed until you crawled out of the sea, you yellow-headed dog. Begone! I did not ask for a parley, and I weary of this babble."

"When I go I'll leave that hovel in ashes!" roared the pirate in a transport of rage. "For the last time- will you give me the loot in return for your lives? I have you hemmed in here, and a hundred men ready to cut your throats."

For answer the Count made a quick gesture with his hand below the points of the palisade. Instantly a matchlock boomed through a loophole and a lock of yellow hair jumped from Harston's head. The pirate yelled vengefully and ran toward the beach, with bullets knocking up the sand behind him. His men roared and came on like a wave, blades gleaming in the sun.

"Curse you, dog!" raved the Count, felling the offending marksman with an iron-clad fist. "W by did you miss'? Ready, men-here they come!"

But Harston had reached his men and checked their headlong rush. The pirates spread out in along line that overlapped the extremities of the western wall, and advanced warily, firing as they came. The heavy bullets smashed into the stockade, and the defenders returned the fire methodically. The women had herded the children into their huts and now stoically awaited whatever fate the gods had in store for them.

The pirates maintained their wide-spread formation, creeping along and taking advantage of every natural depression and bit of vegetation-which was not much, for the ground had been cleared on all sides of the fort against the threat of Indian raids.

A few bodies lay prone on the sandy earth. But the pirates were quick as cats, always shifting their positions and presenting a constantly moving target, hard to hit with the clumsy matchlocks. Their constant raking fire was a continual menace to the men in the stockade. Still, it was evident that as long as the battle remained an exchange of shots, the advantage must remain with the sheltered Frenchmen.

But down at the boat-house on the shore, men were at work with axes. The Count cursed sulphurously when he saw the havoc they were making among his boats, built laboriously of planks sawn from solid logs.

"They're making a mantlet, curse them!" he raged. "A sally now, before they complete it-while they're scattered-"

"We'd be no match for them in hand-to-hand fighting," answered Gallot. "We must keep behind our walls."

"Well enough," growled Henri. "If we can keep them outside!"

Presently the intention of the pirates became apparent, as a group of some thirty men advanced, pushing before them a great shield made out of the planks from the boats and the timbers of the boat-house. They had mounted the mantlet on the wheels of an ox-cart they had found, great solid disks of oak, and as they rolled it ponderously before them the defenders had only glimpses of their moving feet.

"Shoot!" yelled Henri, livid. "Stop them before they reach the gate!"

Bullets smashed into the heavy planks, arrows feathered the thick wood harmlessly. A derisive yell answered the volley. The rest of the pirates were closing in, and their bullets were beginning to find the loop-holes. A soldier fell from the ledge, his skull shattered.

"Shoot at their feet!" screamed Henri, and then: "Forty men at the gate with pikes and axes! The rest hold the wall!"

Bullets ripped into the sand beneath the moving breastwork and some found their mark. But, with a deepthroated shout, the mantlet was pushed to the wall, and an iron-tipped boom, thrust through an aperture in the center of the shield, began to thunder on the gate, driven by muscle-knotted arms. The massive gate groaned and staggered, while from the stockade arrows and bullets poured in a steady hail, and some struck home. But the wild men of the sea were afire with fighting lust. With deep shouts they swung the ram, and from all sides the others closed in, braving the weakened fire from the walls.

23

The Count drew his sword and ran to the gate, cursing like a madman, and a clump of desperate men-at-arms, gripping their pikes, closed in behind him. In another moment the gate would burst asunder and they must stop the gap with their living bodies.

Then a new note entered the clamor of the melee. I t was a trumpet, blaring stridently from the ship. On the crosstrees a figure waved his arms and gesticulated wildly.

The sound registered on Harston's ears, even as he lent his strength to the swinging ram. Bracing his legs to halt the ram on its backward swing, his great thews standing out as he resisted the surge of the other arms, he turned his head, and listened. Sweat dripped from his face.

"Wait!" he roared. "Wait, damn you! Listen!"

In the silence that followed that bull's bellow, the blare of the trumpet was plainly heard, and a voice yelled something which was unintelligible to the people inside the stockade.

But Harston understood, for his voice was lifted again in profane command. The ram was released, and the mantlet began to recede from the gate.

"Look!" cried Tina at her window. "They are running to the beach! They have abandoned the shield! They are leaping into the boats and rowing for the ship! Oh, my Lady, have we won?"

"I think not!" Francoise was staring seaward. "Look!"

She threw aside the curtains and leaned from the window. Her clear young voice rose above the din, turning men's heads in the direction she pointed. They yelled in amazement as they saw another ship swinging majestically around the southern point. Even as they looked, she broke out the lilies of France.

The pirates swarmed up the sides of their ship, then heaved up the anchor. Before the stranger had sailed halfway across the bay, the War-Hawk vanished around the point of the northern horn.

CHAPTER 3

"Out, quick!" snapped the Count, tearing at the bars of the gate. "Destroy that mantlet before these strangers can land!"

"But yonder ship is French!" expostulated Gallot.

"Do as I order!" roared Henri. "My enemies are not all foreigners! Out, dogs, and make kindling of that mantlet!"

Thirty axemen raced down to the beach. They sensed the possibility of peril in the oncoming ship, and there was panic in their haste. The splintering of timbers under their axes came to the ears of the people in the fort, and then the men were racing back across the sands again, as the French ship dropped anchor where the War-Hawk had lain.

"Why does the Count close the gate?" wondered Tina. "Is he afraid that the man he fears might be on that ship?"

"What do you mean, Tina?" Francoise demanded uneasily. The Count had never offered a reason for this self-imposed exile. He was not the sort of a man likely to run from an enemy, though he had many. But this conviction of Tina's was disquieting, almost uncanny.

The child seemed not to have heard her question.

"The axemen are back in the stockade," she said. "The gate is closed again. The men keep their places on the wall. If that ship was chasing Harston, why did it not pursue him? Look, a man is coming ashore. I see a man in the bow, wrapped in a dark cloak."

The boat grounded, and this man came pacing leisurely up the sands, followed by three others. He was tall and wiry, clad in black silk and polished steel.

"Halt!" roared the Count. "I'll parley with your leader, alone!"

The tall stranger removed his morion and made a sweeping bow. His companions halted, drawing their wide cloaks about them, and behind them the sailors leaned on their oars and stared at the palisade.

When he came within easy call of the gate: "Why, surely," said he, "there should be no suspicion between gentlemen." He spoke French without an accent.

The Count stared at him suspiciously. The stranger was dark, with a lean, predatory face, and a thin black mustache. A bunch of lace was gathered at his throat, and there was lace on his wrists.

"I know you," said Henri slowly. "You are Guillaume Villiers."

Again the stranger bowed. "And none could fail to recognize the red falcon of the d'Chastillons."

"It seems this coast has become the rendezvous of all the rogues of the Spanish Main," growled Henri. "What do you want?"

27

"Come, come, sir!" remonstrated Villiers. "This is a churlish greeting to one who has just rendered you a service. Was not that English dog, Harston, thundering at your gate? And did he not take to his sea-heels when he saw me round the point?"

"True," conceded the Count grudgingly. "Though there is little to choose between pirates."

Villiers laughed without resentment and twirled his mustache.

"You are blunt, my lord. I am no pirate. I hold my commission from the governor of Tortuga, to fight the Spaniards. Harston is a sea-thief who holds no commission from any king. I desire only leave to anchor in your bay, to let my men hunt for meat and water in your woods, and, perhaps, myself to drink a glass of wine at your board."

"Very well," growled Henri. "But understand this, Villiers: no man of your crew comes within this stockade. If one approaches closer than a hundred feet, he will immediately find a bullet through his gizzard. And I charge you do no harm to my gardens, or the cattle in the pens. Three steers you may have for fresh meat, but no more."

"I guarantee the good conduct of my men," Villiers assured him. "May they come ashore?"

Henri grudgingly signified his consent, and Villiers bowed, a bit sardonically, and retired with a tread as measured and stately as if he trod the polished floor of Versailles palace, where, indeed, unless rumor lied, he had once been a familiar figure.

"Let no man leave the stockade," Henri ordered Gallot. "His driving Harston from our gate is no guarantee that he would not cut our throats. Many bloody rogues bear the king's commission."

Gallot nodded. The buccaneers were supposed to prey only on the Spaniards; but Villiers had a sinister reputation.

So no one stirred from the palisade while the buccaneers came ashore, sun-burnt men with scarfs bound about their heads and gold hoops in their ears. They camped on the beach, more than a hundred of them, and Villiers posted lookouts on both points. The three beeves designated by Henri, shouting from the wall, were driven forth and slaughtered. Fires were kindled on the strand, and a wattled barrel of wine was brought ashore and broached.

Other kegs were filled with water from the spring that rose a short distance south of the fort, and men began to straggle toward the woods. Seeing this, Henri shouted to Villiers: "Don't let your men go into the forest. Take another steer from the pens if you haven't enough meat. If they go tramping into the woods, they may fall foul of the Indians.

"We beat off an attack shortly after we landed, and since then six of my men have been murdered in the forest, at one time or another. -hhere's peace between us just now, but it hangs by a thread."

Villiers shot a startled glance at the lowering woods, then he bowed and said, "I thank you for the warning, my Lord!" Then he shouted for his men to come back, in a rasping voice that contrasted strangely with his courtly accents when addressing the Count.

If Villiers' eyes could have penetrated that forest wall, he would have been shaken at the appearance of a sinister figure lurking there, one who watched the strangers with resentful black eyes--an unpainted Indian warrior, naked but for a doeskin breech-clout, a hawk feather drooped over his left ear.

As evening drew on, a thin skim of grey crawled tip from the sea-rim and darkened the sky. The sun sank in a wallow of crimson, touching the tips of the black waves with blood. Fog crawled out of the sea and lapped at the feet of the forest, curling about the stockade in smoky wisps. The fires on the beach shone dull crimson through the mist, and the singing of the buccaneers seemed deadened and far away. They had brought old sail-canvas from the ship and made them shelters along the strand, where beef was still roasting, and the wine was doled out sparingly.

The great gate was barred. Soldiers stolidly tramped the ledges of the palisade, pike on shoulder, beads of moisture glistening on their steel caps. They glanced uneasily at the fires on the beach, stared with greater fixity toward the forest, a vague dark line in the fog. The compound lay empty of life. Candles gleamed feebly through the cracks of the huts, light streamed from the windows of the manor building. There was silence except for the tread of the sentries, the drip of the water from the eaves, the distant singing of the buccaneers.

Some faint echo of this singing penetrated into the great hall where Henri sat at wine with his unsolicited guest.

"Your men make merry, sir," grunted the Count.

"They are glad to feel the sand under their feet again," answered Villiers. "It has been a wearisome voyage--yes, a long, stern chase." He lifted his goblet gallantly to the unresponsive girl who sat on his host's right, and drank ceremoniously.

Impassive attendants ranged the walls, soldiers with pikes and helmets, servants in worn satin coats. Henri's household in this wild land was a shadowy reflection of the court he had kept in France.

The manor house, as he insisted on calling it, was a marvel for a savage coast. A hundred men had worked night and day for months building it. The logs that composed the walls of the interior were hidden with heavy silken, goldworked tapestries. Ship beams, stained and polished, formed the support of the lofty ceiling. The floor was covered with rich carpets. The broad stair that led up from the hall was likewise carpeted, and its massive balustrade had once been a galleon's rail.

A fire in the wide stone fireplace dispelled the dampness of the night. Candles in the great silver candelabrum in the center of the broad mahogany board lit the hall, throwing long shadows on the stair. Count Henri sat at the head of that table, presiding over a company composed of his niece, his piratical guest, Gallot, and the captain of the guard.

"You followed Harston?" asked Henri. "You drove him this far afield?"

"I followed Harston," laughed Villiers. "I followed him around the Horn. But he was not fleeing from me. He came seeking something; something I, too, desire."

"What could tempt a pirate to this naked land?" muttered Henri.

"What could tempt a Count of France?" retorted Villiers.

"The rottenness of a royal court might sicken a man of honor."

"D'Chastillons of honor have endured its rottenness for several generations," said Villiers bluntly. "My lord, indulge my curiosity---why did you sell your lands, load your galleon with the furnishings of your castle and sail over the horizon out of the knowledge of men? And why settle here, when your sword and your name might carve out a place for you in any civilized land?"

Henri toyed with the golden seal-chain about his neck.

"As to why I left France," he said, "that is my own affair. But it was chance that left me stranded here. I had brought all my people ashore, and much of the furnishings you mentioned, intending to build a temporary habitation. But my ship, anchored out there in the bay, was driven against the cliffs of the north point and wrecked by a sudden storm out of the west. That left us no way of escape from this spot."

"Then you would return to France, if you could?"

"Not to France. To China, perhaps-or to India-"

"Do you not find it tedious here, my Lady?" asked Villiers, for the first time addressing himself directly to Francoise.

Hunger to see a new face and hear a new voice had brought the girl to the banquet-hall that night. But now she wished she had remained in her chamber with Tina. There was no mistaking the meaning in the glance Villiers turned on her. His speech was decorous, his expression respectful, but it was only a mask through which gleamed the violent and sinister spirit of the man.

"There is little diversion here," she answered in a low voice.

"If you had a ship," Villiers addressed his host, "you would abandon this settlement?"

"Perhaps," admitted the Count.

"I have a ship," said Villiers. "If we could reach an agreement-"

"Agreement?" Henri stared suspiciously at his guest.

"Share and share alike," said Villiers, laying his hand on the board with the fingers spread wide. The gesture was repulsively reminiscent of a great spider. But the fingers quivered with tension, and the buccaneer's eyes burned with a new light.

"Share what?" Henri stared at him in bewilderment. "The gold I brought with me went down in my ship, and unlike the broken timbers, it did not wash ashore."

"Not that!" Villiers made an impatient gesture. "Let us be frank, my lord. Can you pretend it was chance which caused you to land at this particular spot. with thousands of miles of coast to choose from "

"There is no need for me to pretend," answered Henri coldly. "My ship's master was one Jacques Piriou, formerly a buccaneer. He had sailed this coast, and he persuaded me to land here, telling me he had a reason he would later disclose. But this reason he never divulged, because the day we landed he disappeared into the woods, and his headless body was found later by a hunting party. Obviously the Indians slew him."

Villiers stared fixedly at the Count for a space.

"Sink me," quoth he at last. "I believe you, my lord. And I'll make you a proposal. I will admit when I anchored

34

out there in the bay I had other plans in mind. Supposing you to have already secured the treasure, I meant to take this fort by strategy and cut all your throats. But circumstances have caused me to change my mind-" he cast a glance at Francoise that brought color into her face, and made her lift her head indignantly.

"I have a ship to carry you out of exile," said the buccaneer. "But first you must help me secure the treasure."

"What treasure, in Saint Denis' name?" demanded the Count angrily. "You are yammering like that dog Harston, now."

"Did you ever hear of Giovanni da Verrazano?"

"The Italian who sailed as a privateer for France and captured the caravel loaded with Montezuma's treasures which Cortez was sending to Spain?"

"Aye. That was in 1523. The Spaniards claimed to have hanged him in 1527, but they lied. That was the year he sailed over the horizon and vanished from the knowledge of' men. But it was not from the Spaniards that he fled.

"Listen! On that caravel he captured in 1523 was the greatest treasure trove in the world--the jewels of Montezuma! Tales of Aztec gold rang around the world, but Cortez carefully guarded the secret of the gems, for he feared lest the sight should madden his own men to revolt against him. They went aboard ship concealed in a sack of gold dust, and they fell into Verrazano's hands when he took the caravel.

"Like Cortez, da Verrazano kept their possession a secret, save from his officers. He did not share them with his men. He hid them in his cabin, and their glitter got in his blood and drove him mad, as they did with all men who saw them. The secret got out, somehow: perhaps his mates talked. But da Verrazano became obsessed with the fear that other rovers would attack him and loot him of his hoard. Seeking some safe hiding place for the baubles which had come to mean more than his very life, he sailed westward, rounded the Horn, and vanished, nearly a hundred years ago.

"But the tale persists that one man of his crew returned to the Main, only to be captured by the Spaniards. Before he was hanged he told his story and drew a map in his own blood, on parchment, which he smuggled somehow out of his captors' reach. This was the tale he told: da Verrazano sailed northward, until, beyond Darien, beyond the coast of Mexico, he raised a coast where no Christian had ever set foot before.

"In a lonely bay he anchored and went ashore, taking his treasure, and eleven of his most trusted men. Following his orders, the ship sailed northward, to return in a week's time and pick up their captain and his men-for he feared otherwise men he did not trust would spy upon him and learn the hiding place of his trove. In the meantime he meant to hide the treasure in the vicinity of the bay. The ship returned at the appointed time. but there was no trace of da Verrazano and his men, save for the rude dwelling they had built on the beach.

This had been demolished, and there were tracks of naked feet about it, but no sign to show there had been fighting. Nor was there any trace of the treasure, or any sign to show where it was hidden. T he buccaneers plunged into the forest to search for their captain, but were attacked by the savages and driven back to their ship. In despair, they heaved anchor and sailed away, but they were wrecked off the coast of Darien, and only that one man survived.

"That is the tale of the Treasure of da Verrazano, which men have sought in vain for nearly a century. I have seen the map that sailor drew before they hanged him. Harston and Piriou were with me. We looked upon it in a hovel in Havana, where we were skulking in disguise. Somebody knocked over the candle, and somebody howled in the dark, and when we got the light on again, the old miser who owned the map was dead with a d irk in his heart. I he map was gone, and the watch was clattering down tile street with their pikes to investigate the clamor. We scattered, and each went his own way.

"For years thereafter Harston and I watched one another, each thinking the other had the map. Well, as it turned out, neither had it, but recently word came to me that Harston had sailed for the Pacific, so I followed him. You saw the end of that chase.

"I had but a glimpse at the map as it lay on the old miser's table, and could tell nothing about it. But Harston's actions show that he knows this is the bay where da Verrazano anchored. I believe they hid the treasure somewhere in that forest and returning, were attacked and slain by the savages. The Indians did not get the treasure. Neither Cabrillo nor Drake, nor any man who ever touched this coast ever saw any gold or jewels in the hands of the Indians.

"This is my proposal: let us combine our forces. Harston fled because he feared to be pinned between us, but he will return. If we are allied, we can laugh at him. We can work out from the fort, leaving enough men here to hold it if he attacks. I believe the treasure is hidden near by. We will find it and sail for some port of Germany or Italy where I can cover my past with gold. I'm sick of this life. I want to go back to Europe and live like a noble, with riches, and slaves, and a castle-and a wife of noble blood."

"Well?" demanded the Count, slit-eyed with suspicion.

"Give me your niece for my wife," demanded the buccaneer bluntly. Francoise cried out sharply and started to her feet. Henri likewise rose, livid. Villiers did not move. H is fingers on the table hooked like talons, and his eyes smoldered with passion and a deep menace.

"You dare!" ejaculated Henri.

"You forget you have fallen from your high estate, Count Henri," growled Villiers. "We are not at Versailles, my lord. On this naked coast nobility is measured by the power of men and arms. And there I rank you. Strangers tread d'Chastillon Castle, and the d'Chastillon fortune is at the bottom of the sea. You will die here, an exile, unless I give you the use of my ship.

"You will have no cause to regret the union of our houses. With a new name and a new fortune you will find that Guillaume Villiers can take his place among the nobility of the world, and make a son-in-law of which not even a d'Chastillon need be ashamed."

"You are mad!" exclaimed the Count violently. "You—what is that?"

It was the patter of soft-slippered feet. Tina came hurriedly into the hall, curtsied timidly, and sidled around the table to thrust her small hands into Francoise's fingers. She was panting slightly, her slippers were damp, and her flaxen hair was plastered wetly on her head.

"Tina! Where have you been? I thought you were in your chamber!"

"I was," answered the child breathlessly, "but I missed my coral necklace you gave me—"She held it up, a trivial trinket, but prized beyond all her other possessions because it had been Francoise's first gift to her. "I was afraid you wouldn't let me go if you knew-a soldier's wife helped me out of the stockade and back again. I found my necklace by the pool where I bathed this morning. Please punish me if I have done wrong."

"Tina!" groaned Francoise, clasping the child to her. "I'm not going to punish you. But you should not have gone outside the stockade. Let me take you to your chamber and change these damp clothes--"

"Yes, my Lady," murmured Tina, "but first let me tell you about the black man-"

"What?" It was a cry that burst from Count Henri's lips. His goblet clattered to the floor as he caught the table with both hands. If a thunderbolt had struck him, his bearing could not have been more horrifyingly altered. His face was livid, his eyes starting from his head.

"What did you say`'" he panted. "What did you say, wench?"

"A black man, my lord," she stammered, while all stared at Henri in amazement "When I went down to the pool to get my necklace, I saw him. I was afraid and hid behind a ridge of sand. He came from the sea in an open boat. He drew the boat up on the sands below the south point, and strode toward the forest, looking like a giant in the fog, a great, tall black man="

Henri reeled as if he had received a mortal blow. He clutched at his throat, snapping the golden chain in his violence. With the face of a madman he lurched about the table and tore the child screaming from Francoise's arms.

"You lie!" he panted. "You lie to torment me! Say that you lie before I tear the skin from your back!"

"Uncle!" cried Francoise, trying to free Tina from his grasp. "Are you mad? What are you about?"

With a snarl he tore her hand from his arm and spun her staggering into the arms of Gallot who received her with a leer he did not conceal.

"Mercy, my lord!" sobbed Tina. "I did not lie!"

"I say you lied!" roared Henri. "Jacques!"

A stolid serving man seized the shivering youngster and tore the garments from her back with one brutal wrench. Wheeling, he drew her slender arms over his shoulders, lifting her feet clear of the floor.

"Uncle!" shrieked Francoise, writhing vainly in Gallot's grasp. "You are mad! You can not---oh, you can not-!" The cry choked in her throat as Henri caught up a Jewel-hilted riding whip and brought it down across the child's frail body with a savagery that left a red weal across her naked shoulders.

Francoise went sick with the anguish in Tina's shriek. The world had suddenly gone mad. As if in a nightmare she saw the stolid faces of the retainers, reflecting neither pity nor sympathy. Villiers' sneering face was part of the nightmare. Nothing in that crimson haze was real except

Tina's naked white shoulders, crisscrossed with red welts; no sound real except the child's sharp cries of agony, and the panting gasps of Henri as he lashed away with the staring eyes of a madman, shrieking: "You lie! Admit your guilt, or I will flay you! He could not have followed me here-"

"Mercy, mercy, my lord!" screamed the child, writhing vainly on the brawny servant's back. "I saw him! I do not lie! Please! Please!"

"You fool! You fool!" screamed Francoise, almost beside herself. "Do you not see she is telling the truth? Oh, you beast! Beast! Beast!"

Suddenly some shred of sanity seemed to return to Henri's brain. Dropping the whip he reeled back and fell up against the table, clutching blindly at its edge. He shook as if with an ague. H is hair was plastered across his brow in dank strands, and sweat dripped from his livid countenance which was like a carven mask of Fear. Tina, released by Jacques, slipped to the floor in a whimpering heap. Francoise tore free from Gallot, rushed to her, sobbing, and fell on her knees, gathering the pitiful waif into her arms. She lifted a terrible face to her uncle, to pour upon him the full vials of her wrath--but he was not looking at her. In a daze of incredulity, she heard him say: "I accept your offer, Villiers. In God's name, let us find your treasure and begone from this accursed coast!"

At this the fire of her fury sank to sick ashes. In stunned silence she lifted the sobbing child in her arms and carried her up the stair. A backward glance showed Henri crouching rather than sitting at the table, gulping wine from a goblet he gripped in both shaking hands, while Villiers towered over him like a somber predatory bird-puzzled at the turn of events, but quick to take advantage of the shocking change that had come over the Count. He was talking in a low, decisive voice, and Henri nodded mute agreement, like one who scarcely heeds what is being said. Gallot stood back in the shadows, chin pinched between forefinger and thumb, and the retainers along the walls glanced furtively at each other, bewildered by their lord's collapse.

Up in her chamber Francoise laid the half-fainting girl on the bed and set herself to wash and apply soothing ointments to the weals and cuts on the child's tender skin. Tina gave herself up in complete submission to her mistress's hands, moaning faintly. Francoise felt as if her world had fallen about her ears. She was sick and bewildered, overwrought, her nerves quivering from the brutal shock of what she had witnessed. Fear and hate of her uncle grew in her soul. She had never loved him; he was harsh and without affection, grasping and avid. But she had considered him just and courageous. Revulsion shook her at the memory of his staring eyes and bloodless face. It was some terrible fear which had roused this frenzy; and because of this fear Henri had brutalized the only creature she had to love; because of that fear he was selling her, his niece, to an infamous outlaw. What was behind this madness?

The child muttered in semi-delirium.

"Indeed, I did not lie, my Lady! I saw him-a black man, wrapped in a black cloak! My blood ran cold when I saw him. Why did the Count whip me for seeing him?"

"Hush, Tina," soothed Francoise. "Lie quiet, child."

The door opened behind her and she whirled, snatching up a jeweled dagger. Henri stood in the door, and her flesh crawled at the sight of him. He looked years older; his face was grey and drawn, his eyes made her shiver. She had never been close to him; now she felt as though a gulf separated them. He was not her uncle who stood there, but a stranger come to menace her.

She lifted the dagger.

"If you touch her again," she whispered from dry lips, "I swear I will sink this blade in your breast."

He did not heed her threat.

"I have posted a strong guard about the manor," he said. "Villiers brings his men into the stockade tomorrow. He will not sail until he has found the treasure. When he finds it we sail."

"And you will sell me to him?" she whispered. "In God's name

He fixed upon her a gloomy gaze from which all considerations but his own self-interest had been crowded out. She shrank before it, seeing in it the frantic cruelty that possessed the man in his mysterious fear.

"You will do as I command," he said presently, with no more human feeling in his voice than there is in the ring of flint on steel. And turning, he left the chamber. Blinded by a sudden rush of horror, Francoise fell fainting beside the couch where Tina lay.

CHAPTER 4

Francoise never knew how long she lay crushed and senseless. She was first aware of Tina's arms about her and the sobbing of the child in her ear. Mechanically she straightened herself and drew the girl into her arms. She sat there, dry-eyed, staring unseeingly at the flickering candle. There was no sound in the castle. The singing of the buccaneers on the strand had ceased. Dully she reviewed her problem.

Clearly, the story of the mysterious black man had driven Henri mad and it was to escape this man that he meant to abandon the settlement and flee with Villiers. That much was obvious. Equally obvious was the fact that he was ready to sacrifice her for that opportunity to escape. In the blackness which surrounded her, she saw no glint of light. The serving men were dull or callous brutes, their women stupid and apathetic. They would neither dare nor care to help her. She was utterly helpless.

Tina lifted her tear-stained face as if listening to the prompting of some inner voice. The child's understanding of Francoise's inmost thoughts was almost uncanny, as was her recognition of the inexorable drive of Fate and the only alternative left them.

"We must go, my Lady!" she whispered. "Villiers shall not have you. Let us go far away into the forest. We shall go until we can go no further, and then we shall lie down and die together."

The tragic strength that is the last refuge of the weak entered Francoise's soul. It was the only escape from the shadows that had been closing in upon her since that day when they fled from France.

"We shall go, child."

She rose and was fumbling for a cloak, when an exclamation from Tina brought her about. The child was on her feet, a finger pressed to her lips, her eyes wide and bright with sudden terror.

"What is it, Tina?" Francoise whispered, seized by a nameless dread.

"Someone outside in the hall," whispered Tina, clutching her arm convulsively. "He stopped at our door, and then went on down the hall."

"Your ears are keener than mine," murmured Francoise. "But there's nothing strange in that. It was the Count, perchance, or Gallot."

She moved to open the door, but Tina threw her arms about her neck, and Francoise could feel the wild beating of her heart.

"Do not open the door, my Lady! I am afraid! Some evil thing is near!"

Impressed, Francoise reached a hand toward the metal disk that masked a tiny peep-hole in the door.

"He is coming back!" shivered the girl. "I hear him."

Francoise heard something too -a stealthy pad which she realized, with a chill of fear, was not the step of anyone she knew. Nor was it the tread of Villiers, or any booted man. But who could it be? None slept upstairs besides herself, Tina, the Count, and Gallot.

With a quick motion she extinguished the candle so it would not shine through the hole in the door, and pushed aside the metal disk. Staring through she sensed rather than saw a dim bulk moving past her door, but she could make nothing of its shape except that it was manlike. But a blind unreasoning terror froze her tongue to her palate.

The figure passed on to the stairhead, where it was limned momentarily against the faint glow that came up from below--a vague, monstrous image, black against the red-then it was gone down the stair. She crouched in the darkness, awaiting some outcry to announce that the soldiers on guard had sighted the intruder. But the fort remained silent; somewhere a wind wailed shrilly. That was all.

Francoise's hands were moist with perspiration as she groped to relight the candle. She did not know just what there had been about that black figure etched against the red glow of the fireplace below that had roused such horror in her soul. But she knew she had seen something sinister and grisly beyond comprehension, and that the sight had robbed her of all her new-found resolution. She was demoralized.

The candle flared up, limning Tina's white face in the grow.

"It was the black man!" whispered Tina. "I know! My blood turned cold just as it did when I saw him on the beach! Shall we go and tell the Count?"

Francoise shook her head. She did not wish a repetition of what had occurred at Tina's first mention of the black invader. At any event, she dared not venture into that darkened hallway. She knew men were patrolling the stockade, and were stationed outside the manor house. How the stranger had got into the fort she could not guess. It smacked of the diabolical. But she began to have a strong intuition that the creature was no longer within the fortress; that he had departed as mysteriously as he had come.

"We dare not go into the forest!" shuddered Tina. "He will be lurking there..."

Francoise did not ask the girl how she knew the black man would be in the forest; it was the logical hiding place for any evil thing, man or devil. And she knew Tina was right. They dared not leave the fort now. Her determination which had not faltered at the prospect of certain death, gave way at the thought of traversing those gloomy woods with that black shambling creature at large among them. Helplessly she sat down and covered her face with her hands.

Finally, Tina slept, whimpering occasionally in her sleep. Tears gleamed on her long lashes. She moved her smarting body restlessly. 'Toward dawn, Francoise was aware that the atmosphere had become stifling. She heard a low rumble of thunder off to seaward. Extinguishing the candle, which had burned to its socket, she went to a window whence she could see both the ocean and a belt of the forest.

The fog had disappeared, but out to sea a dusky mass was rising from the horizon. From it lightning flickered and low thunder growled. Then an answering rumble came from the black woods. Startled, she turned and stared at the forest. A rhythmic pulsing reached her ears-a droning reverberation that was not the thumping of an Indian drum.

"The drum!" sobbed Tina, spasmodically opening and closing her fingers in her sleep. "The black man-beating on a black drum--in the black woods! Oh, save us!"

Francoise shuddered. Along the eastern horizon ran a thin white line that presaged dawn. But that black cloud on the western rim expanded swiftly. She watched in surprise, for storms were practically unknown on that coast at that time of year, and she had never seen such a cloud.

It came pouring up over the world-rim in great boiling masses of fire-veined blackness. It rolled and billowed with the wind in its belly. Its thundering made the air vibrate. And another sound mingled awesomely with the thunder-the voice of the wind, that raced before its coming. The inky horizon was torn and convulsed in the lightning flashes; far at sea she saw the white-capped waves racing before the wind. She heard its droning roar, rising in volume as it swept shoreward. But as yet no wind stirred on the land. The air was hot, breathless. Somewhere below her a shutter slammed, and a woman's voice was lifted, shrill with alarm. But the manor still slumbered.

She still heard that mysterious drum droning, and her flesh crawled. The forest was a black rampart her sight could not penetrate, but she visualized a hideous black figure squatting under black branches and smiting incessantly on a drum gripped between its knees. But why?

She shook off her ghoulish conviction and looked seaward as a blaze of lightning split the sky. Outlined against the glare she saw the masts of Villiers' ship, the tents on the beach, the sandy ridges of the south point and the rocky cliffs of the north point. Louder and louder rose the roar of the wind, and now the manor was awake. Feet came pounding up the stair, and Villiers' voice yelled, edged with fright.

Doors slammed and Henri answered him, shouting to make himself heard.

"Why didn't you warn me of a storm from the west?" howled the buccaneer. "If the anchors don't hold she'll drive on the rocks!"

"A storm never came from the west before at this time of year!" shrieked Henri, rushing from his chamber in his night shirt, his face white and his hair standing on end. "This is the work of-" His words were drowned as he raced

51

up the ladder that led to the lookout tower, followed by the swearing buccaneer.

Francoise crouched at her window, awed and deafened. The wind drowned all other sound-all except that maddening droning which rose now like a chant of triumph. It roared inshore, driving before it a foaming league long crest of white--and then all hell was loosed on that coast. Rain swept the beaches in driving torrents. The wind hit like a thunder-clap, making the timbers of the fort quiver. The surf roared over the sands, drowning the coals of the seamen's fires. In the lightning glare Francoise saw, through the curtain of the slashing rain, the tents of the buccaneers ripped to ribbons and washed away, saw the men themselves staggering toward the fort, beaten almost to the sands by the fury of torrent and blast.

And limned against the blue glare she saw Villiers' ship, ripped loose from her moorings, driven headlong against the jagged cliffs that jutted up to receive her.

CHAPTER 5

The storm had spent its fury, and the sun shone in a clear blue, rain-washed sky. At a small stream which wound among trees and bushes to join the sea, an Englishman bent to lave his hands and face. He performed his ablutions after the manner of his race, grunting and splashing like a buffalo. In the midst of these splashings he lifted his head suddenly, his tawny hair dripping and water running in rivulets over his brawny shoulders. All in one motion he was on his feet and facing inland, sword in hand.

A man as big as himself was striding toward him over the sands, a cutlass in his hand and unmistakable purpose in his approach.

The pirate paled, as recognition blazed in his eyes.

"Satan!" he ejaculated unbelievingly. "You!"

Oaths streamed from his lips as he heaved up his cutlass. The birds rose in flaming showers from the trees, frightened at the clang of steel. Blue sparks flew from the hacking blades, and the sand ground under the stamping boot heels. Then the clangor ended in a chopping crunch, and one man went to his knees with a choking gasp. The hilt escaped his hand, and he slid to the reddened sand. With a dying effort he fumbled at his girdle and drew something from it, tried to lift it to his mouth, and then stiffened convulsively and went limp.

The conqueror bent and tore the stiffening fingers from the object they crumpled in their desperate grasp.

Villiers and d'Chastillon stood on the beach, staring at the spars, shattered masts and broken timbers their men were gathering. So savagely had the storm hammered Villiers' ship against the low cliffs that most of the salvage was match-wood. A short distance behind them stood Francoise, with one arm about Tina. The girl was pale and listless, apathetic to whatever Fate held in store for her. She listened to the conversation without interest. She was crushed by the realization that she was but a pawn in the game, however it was to be played out.

Villiers cursed venomously, but Henri seemed dazed.

"This is not the time of year for storms," he muttered. "It was not chance that brought that storm out of the deep to splinter the ship in which I meant to escape. Escape? Nay, we are all trapped rats."

"I don't know what you're talking about," snarled Villiers. "I've been unable to get any sense out of you since that flaxen-haired hussy upset you so last night with her wild tale of black men coming out of the sea. But I know that I'm not going to spend my life on this cursed coast. Ten of my men drowned with the ship, but I've got a hundred more. You've got nearly as many. There are tools in your fort and plenty of trees in yonder forest. We'll build some kind of a craft that will carry us until we can take a ship from the Spaniards."

"It will take months," muttered Henri.

"Well, is there any better way in which we could employ our time? We're here-and we'll get away only by our own efforts. I hope that storm smashed Harston to bits! While we're building our craft we'll hunt for da Verrazano's treasure."

"We will never complete your ship," said Henri somberly.

"You fear the Indians? We have men enough to defy them."

"I do not speak of red men. I speak of a black man."

Villiers turned on him angrily. "Will you talk sense? Who is this accursed black man?"

"Accursed indeed," said Henri, staring seaward. "Through fear of him I fled from France, hoping to drown my trail in the western ocean. But he has smelled me out in spite of all."

"If such a man came ashore he must be hiding in the woods," growled Villiers. "We'll rake the forest and hunt him out."

Henri laughed harshly.

"Grope in the dark for a cobra with your naked hand!"

Villiers cast him an uncertain look, obviously doubting his sanity.

"Who is this man? Have done with ambiguity."

"A devil spawned on that coast of hell, the Slave Coast-"

"Sail ho!" bawled the lookout on the north point.

Villiers wheeled and his voice slashed the wind.

"Do you know her?"

"Aye!" the reply came back faintly. "It's the War-Hawk!"

"Harston!" raged Villiers. "The devil takes care of his own! How could he ride out that blow?" His voice rose to a yell that carried up and down the strand. "Back to the fort, you dogs!"

Before the War-Hawk, somewhat battered in appearance, nosed around the point, the beach was bare of human life, the palisade bristling with helmets and scarf-bound heads. Villiers ground his teeth as a long-boat swung into the beach and Harston strode toward the fort alone.

"Ahoy the fort!" The Englishman's bull bellow carried clearly in the still morning. "I want to parley! The last time I advanced under a flag of truce I was fired upon! I want a promise that it won't happen again."

"All right, I'll give you my promise!" called Villiers sardonically.

"Damn your promise, you French dog! I want d'Chastillon's word."

A measure of dignity remained to the Count. There was an edge of authority to his voice as he answered: "Advance, but keep your men back. You will not be fired upon."

"That's enough for me," said Harston instantly. "Whatever a d'Chastillon's sins, once his word is given, you can trust him."

He strode forward and halted under the gate, laughing at the hate-darkened visage Villiers thrust over at him.

"Well, Guillaume," he taunted, "you are a ship shorter than when last I saw you! But you French never were sailors."

"How did you save your ship, you Bristol gutterscum?" snarled the buccaneer.

"There's a cove some miles to the north protected by a high-ridged arm of land that broke the force of the gale," answered Harston. "I lay behind it. My anchors dragged, but they held me off the shore."

Villiers scowled at Henri, who said nothing. The Count had not known of that cove. He had done little exploring of his domain, fear of the Indians keeping him and his men near the fort.

"I've come to make a trade," said Harston easily.

"We've naught to trade with you save sword-strokes," growled Villiers.

"I think otherwise," grinned Harston, thin-lipped. "You tipped your hand when you murdered Richardson, my first mate, and robbed him. Until this morning I supposed that d'Chastillon had da Verrazano's treasure. But if either of you had it, you wouldn't have gone to the trouble of following me and killing my mate to get the map."

"The map!" ejaculated Villiers, stiffening.

"Oh, don't dissemble!" Harston laughed, but anger blazed blue in his eyes. "I know you have it. Indians don't wear boots!"

"But--" began Henri, nonplussed, but fell silent as Villiers nudged him.

"What have you to trade?" Villiers demanded of Harston.

"Let me come into the fort," suggested the pirate. "We can talk there."

"Your men will stay where they are," warned Villiers.

"Aye. But don't think you'll seize me and hold me for a hostage!" He laughed grimly. "I want d'Chastillon's word that I'll be allowed to leave the fort alive and unhurt within the hour, whether we come to terms or not."

"You have my pledge," answered the Count.

"All right, then. Open that gate."

The gate opened and closed, the leaders vanished from sight, and the common men of both parties resumed their silent surveillance of each other.

On the broad stair above the hall, Francoise and Tina crouched, ignored by the men below. Henri, Gallot, Villiers and Harston sat about the broad table. Except for them the hall was empty.

Harston gulped wine and set the empty goblet on the table. The frankness suggested by his bluff countenance was belied by the lights of cruelty and treachery in his wide eyes. But he spoke bluntly enough.

"We all want the treasure da Verrazano hid somewhere near this bay," he said. "Each has something the others need. D'Chastillon has laborers, supplies, a stockade to shelter us from the savages. You, Villiers, have my map. I have a ship."

"If you had the map all these years," said Villiers, "why didn't you come after the loot sooner?"

"I didn't have it. It was Piriou who knifed the old miser in the dark and stole the map. But he had neither ship nor crew, and it took him more than a year to get them. When he did come after the loot, the Indians prevented his landing, and his men mutinied and made him sail back to the Main. One of them stole the map, and later sold it to me."

"That was why Piriou recognized the bay," muttered Henri.

"Did that dog lead you here? I might have guessed it. Where is he?"

"Slain by Indians, evidently while searching for the treasure."

"Good!" approved Harston heartily. "Well, I don't know how you knew my mate was carrying the map. I trusted him, and the men trusted him more than they did me, so I let him keep it. But this morning he wandered in and got separated from the rest, and we found him sworded to death near the beach, and the map gone. The men accused me of killing him, but we found the tracks left by the man who killed him, and I showed the fools my feet wouldn't fit them. There wasn't a boot in the crew that made that sort of track. Indians don't wear boots. So it had to be a Frenchman.

"You've got the map, but you haven't got the treasure. If you had it, you wouldn't have let me in the fort. I've got you penned up here. You can't get out to look for the loot, and no ship to carry it away, anyhow.

"Here's my proposal: Villiers, give me the map. And you, Count, give me fresh meat and supplies. My men are nigh to scurvy after the long voyage. In return I'll take you three men, the Lady Francoise and her girl, and set you ashore at some port of the Atlantic where you can take ship to France. And to clinch the bargain, I'll give each of you a handsome share in the treasure."

The buccaneer tugged his mustache meditatively. He knew that Harston would not keep any such pact, if made. Nor did Villiers even consider agreeing to the proposal. But to refuse bluntly would be to force the issue into a clash of arms, and Villiers was not ready for that. He wanted the War-Hawk as avidly as he desired the jewels of Montezuma.

"What's to prevent us from holding you captive and forcing your men to give us your ship in exchange for you'?" he asked.

Harston laughed at him.

"Do you think I'm a fool? My men have orders to heave up the anchors and sail hence at the first hint of treachery. They wouldn't give you the ship, if you skinned me alive on the beach. Besides, I have Henri's word."

"My word is not wind," said Henri somberly. "Have done with threats, Villiers."

The buccaneer did not reply, his mind being wholly absorbed in the problem of getting possession of Harston's ship; of continuing the parley without betraying the fact that he did not have the map. He wondered who in Satan's name did have the accursed map.

"Let me take my men away with me on your ship," he said. "I can not desert my faithful followers-"

Harston snorted.

"Why don't you ask for my cutlass to cut my throat with? Desert your faithful-bah! You'd desert your brother to the devil if it meant money in your pocket. No! You're not going to bring enough men aboard to mutiny and take my ship."

"Give us a day to think it over," urged Villiers, fighting for time.

Harston's heavy fist banged on the table, making the wine dance in the glasses.

"No, by Satan! Give me my answer now!"

Villiers was on his feet, his black rage submerging his craftiness.

"You English dog! I'll give you your answer-in your guts!"

He tore aside his cloak, caught at his sword hilt. Harston heaved up with a roar, his chair crashing backward to the floor. Henri sprang up, spreading his arms between them as they faced each other across the board.

"Gentlemen, have done! Villiers, he has my pledge-"

"The foul fiend gnaw your pledge!" snarled Villiers.

"Stand from between us, my lord," growled the pirate, his voice thick with the killing lust. "I release you from your word until I have slain this dog!"

"Well spoken, Harston!" It was a deep, powerful voice behind them, vibrant with grim amusement. All wheeled and glared open-mouthed. Up on the stair Francoise started up with an involuntary exclamation.

A man strode out from the hangings that masked a chamber door, and advanced toward the table without haste or hesitation. Instantly he dominated the group, and all felt the situation subtly charged with a new, dynamic atmosphere.

The stranger was as tall as either of the freebooters, and more powerfully built than either, yet for all his size he moved with a pantherish suppleness in his flaring-topped boots. His thighs were cased in close-fitting breeches of white silk, his wide-skirted sky-blue coat open to reveal a white silken shirt beneath, and the scarlet sash that girdled his waist. There were silver acorn-shaped buttons on the coat, and it was adorned with gilt-worked cuffs and pocketflaps, and a satin collar. A broad brimmed, plumed hat was on the stranger's head, and a heavy cutlass hung at his hip.

"Vulmea!" ejaculated Harston, and the others caught their breath.

"Who else?" The giant strode up to the table, laughing sardonically at their amazement.

"What-what do you here?" stuttered Gallot.

"I climbed the palisade on the east side while you fools were arguing at the gate," Vulmea answered. His Irish accent was faint, but not to be mistaken. "Every man in the fort was craning his neck westward. I entered the house while Harston was being let in at the gate. I've been in that chamber there ever since, eavesdropping."

"I thought you were drowned," said Villiers slowly. "Three years ago the shattered hull of your ship was sighted off the coast of Amichel, and you were seen no more on the Main."

"But I live, as you see," retorted Vulmea.

Up on the stair Tina was staring through the balustrades with all her eyes, clutching Francoise in her excitement.

"Vulmea! It is Black Vulmea, my Lady! Look! Look!"

Francoise was looking. It was like encountering a legendary character in the flesh. Who of all the sea-folk had not heard the tales and ballads celebrating the wild deeds of Black Vulmea, once a scourge of the Spanish Main'? The man could not be ignored. Irresistibly he had stalked into the scene, to form another, dominant element in the tangled plot.

Henri was recovering from the shock of finding a stranger in his hall. "What do you want?" he demanded. "Did you come from the sea?"

"I came from the woods," answered the Irishman. "And I gather there is some dissension over a map!"

"That's none of your affair," growled Harston.

"Is this it?" Grinning wickedly, Vulmea drew from his pocket a crumpled object--a square of parchment, marked with crimson lines.

Harston started violently, paling.

"My map!" he ejaculated. "Where did you get it?"

"From Richardson, after I killed him!" was the grim answer.

"You dog!" raved Harston, turning on Villiers. "You never had the map! You lied--"

"I never said I had it," snarled the Frenchman. "You deceived yourself. Don't be a tool. Vulmea is alone. If he had a crew he'd have cut our throats already. We'll take the map from him--"

"You'll never touch it!" Vulmea laughed fiercely.

Both men sprang at him, cursing. Stepping back he crumpled the parchment and cast it into the glowing coals of the fireplace. With a bellow Harston lunged past him, to be met with a buffet under the ear that stretched him half-senseless on the floor. Villiers whipped out his sword, but before he could thrust Vulmea's cutlass beat it out of his hand.

Villiers staggered against the table, with hell in his eyes. Harston lurched to his feet, blood dripping from his ear.

Vulmea leaned over the table, his outstretched blade just touching Count Henri's breast.

"Don't call for your soldiers, Count," said the Irishman softly. "Not a sound out of you, either, dog-face!" His name for Gallot, who showed no intention of disobeying. "The map's burned to ashes, and it'll do no good to spill blood. Sit down, all of you."

Harston hesitated, then shrugged his shoulders and sank sullenly into a chair. The others followed suit. Vulmea stood, towering over the table, while his enemies watched him with bitter eyes of hate.

"You were bargaining," he said. "That's all I've come to do."

"And what have you to trade?" sneered Villiers.

"The jewels of Montezuma!"

"What?" All four men were on their feet, leaning toward him.

"Sit down!" he roared, banging his broad blade on the table. They sank back, tense and white with excitement. He grinned hardly.

"Yes! I found it before I got the map. That's why I burned the map. I don't need it. And now nobody will ever find it, unless I show him where it is."

They stared at him with murder in their eyes, and Villiers said: "You're lying. You've told us one lie already. You say you came from the woods, yet all men know this country is a wilderness, inhabited only by savages."

"And I've been living for three years with those same savages," retorted Vulmea. "When a gale wrecked my ship near the mouth of the Rio Grande, I swam ashore and fled inland and northward, to escape the Spaniards. I fell in with a wandering tribe of Indians who were drifting westward to escape a stronger tribe, and nothing better offering itself, I lived with them and shared their wanderings until a month ago.

"By this time our rovings had brought us so far westward I believed I could reach the Pacific Coast, so I set forth alone. But a hundred miles to the east I encountered a hostile tribe of red men, who would have burned me alive, if I hadn't killed their war-chief and three or four others and broken away one night.

"They chased me to within a few miles of this coast, where I finally shook them off. And by Satan, the place where I took refuge turned out to be the treasure trove of da Verrazano! I found it all: chests of garments and weapons-that's where I clothed and armed myself-heaps of gold and silver, and in the midst of all the jewels of Montezuma gleaming like frozen starlight! And da Verrazano and his eleven buccaneers sitting about an ebon table as they've sat for nearly a hundred years!"

"What?"

"Aye! They died in the midst of their treasure! Their bodies have shrivelled but not rotted. They sit there with their wine glasses in their stiff hands, just as they have sat for nearly a century!"

"That's an unchancy thing!" muttered Harston uneasily, but Villiers snarled: "What boots it? It's the loot we want. Go on, Vulmea."

Vulmea seated himself and filled a goblet before he resumed: "I lay up and rested a few days, made snares to catch rabbits, and let my wounds heal. I saw smoke against the western sky, but thought it some Indian village on the beach. I lay close, but the loot's hidden in a place the redskins shun. If any spied on me, they didn't show themselves.

"Last night I started for the beach, meaning to strike it some miles north of the spot where I'd seen the smoke. I was close to the shore when the storm hit. I took shelter under a big rock, and when it had blown itself out, I climbed a tree to look for Indians. Then I saw your ship at anchor, Harston, and your men coming in to shore. I was making my way toward your camp on the beach when I met Richardson. I killed him because of an old quarrel. I wouldn't have known he had a map if he hadn't tried to eat it before he died.

"I recognized it, of course, and was considering what use I could make of it, when the rest of you dogs came up and found the body. I was lying in a thicket close by while you were arguing with your men about the killing. I judged the time wasn't ripe for me to show myself then"

-He laughed at the rage displayed in Harston's face.

"Well, while I lay there listening to your talk, I got a drift of the situation and learned, from the things you let fall, that d'Chastillon and Villiers were a few miles south on the beach. So when I heard you say that Villiers must have done the killing and taken the map, and that you meant to parley with him, seeking an opportunity to murder him and get it back-"

"Dog!" snarled Villiers.

Harston was livid, but he laughed mirthlessly.

"Do you think I'd deal fair with a dog like you? Go on, Vulmea."

The Irishman grinned. It was evident that he was deliberately fanning the fires of hate between the two men.

"Nothing much, then I came straight through the woods while you were beating along the coast, and raised the fort before you did. And there's the tale. I have the treasure, Harston has a ship, Henri has supplies. By Satan, Villiers, I don't see where you fit in, but to avoid strife I'll include you. My proposal is simple enough.

"We'll split the loot four ways. Harston and I will sail away with our shares aboard the War-Hunk. You and d'Chastillon take yours and remain lords of the wilderness, or build a ship out of logs, as you wish."

Henri blenched arid Villiers swore, while Harston grinned quietly.

"Are you fool enough to go aboard the War-Hawk with Harston?" snarled Villiers. "He'll cut your throat before you're out of sight of land!"

"This is like the problem of the sheep, the wolf and the cabbage," laughed Vulmea. "How to get them across the river without their devouring each other!"

"And that appeals to your Celtic sense of humor," complained Villiers.

"I will not stay here!" cried Henri. "Treasure or no, I must go!"

Vulmea gave him a slit-eyed glance of speculation.

"Well, then," said he, "let Harston sail away with Villiers, yourself, and such members of your household as you may select, leaving me in command of the fort and the rest of your men, and all of Villiers'. I'll build a boat that will get me into Spanish waters."

Villiers looked slightly sick.

"I am to have the choice of remaining here in exile, or abandoning my crew and going alone on the War-Hawk to have my throat cut?"

Vulmea's gusty laughter boomed through the hall, and he smote Villiers jovially on the back, ignoring the black murder in the buccaneer's glare.

"That's it, Guillaume!" quoth he. "Stay here while Dick and I sail away, or sail away with Dick, leaving your men with me."

"I'd rather have Villiers," said Harston frankly. "You'd turn my own men against me, Vulmea, and cut my throat before I rounded the Horn."

Sweat dripped from Villiers' face.

"Neither I, the Count, nor his niece will ever reach France alive if we ship with that devil," said he. "You are both in my power now. My men surround this hall. What's to prevent me cutting you both down?"

"Nothing," admitted Vulmea cheerfully. "Except that if you do Harston's men will sail away with the ship and that with me dead you'll never find the treasure; and that I'll split your skull if you summon your men."

Vulmea laughed as he spoke, but even Francoise sensed that he meant what he said. His naked cutlass lay across his knees, and Villiers' sword was under the table, out of reach.

"Aye!" said Harston with an oath. "You'd find the two of us no easy prey. I'm agreeable to Vulmea's offer. What do you say, my lord?"

` I must leave this coast!" whispered Henri, staring blankly. "I must hasten. I must go far-go quickly!"

Harston frowned, puzzled at the Count's strange manner, and turned to Villiers, grinning wickedly: "And you Guillaume?"

"What choice have I?" snarled Villiers. "Let me take my three officers and forty men aboard the War-Hawk, and the bargain's made."

"The officers and fifteen men!"

"Very well."

"Done!"

There was no shaking of hands to seal the pact. The two captains glared at each other like hungry wolves. The Count plucked his mustache with a trembling hand, rapt in his own somber thoughts. Vulmea drank wine and grinned on the assemblage, but it was the grin of a stalking tiger.

71

Francoise sensed the murderous purposes that reigned there, the treacherous intent that dominated each man's mind. Not one had any intention of keeping his part of the pact, Henri possibly excluded. Each of the freeboaters intended to possess both the ship and the entire treasure. Neither would be satisfied with less. But what was going on in each crafty mind? Francoise felt oppressed by the atmosphere of hatred and treachery. The Irishman, for all his savage frankness, was no less subtle than the others-and even fiercer. His gigantic shoulders and massive limbs seemed too big even for the great hall. There was an iron vitality about the man that overshadowed even the hard vigor of the other freebooters.

"Lead us to the treasure!" Villiers demanded.

"Wait a bit," returned Vulmea. "We must keep our power evenly balanced, so one can't take advantage of the others. This is what we'll do: Harston's men will come ashore, all but half a dozen or so, and camp on the beach. Villiers' men will come out of the fort and likewise camp on the beach, within easy sight of them. Then each crew can keep a check on the other, to see that nobody slips after us who go after the treasure. Those left aboard the War-Hawk will take her out into the bay out of reach of either party. Henri's men will stay in the fort, but leave the gate open. Will you come with us, Count?"

"Go into that forest?" Henri shuddered, and drew his cloak about his shoulders. "Not for all the gold of Mexico!"

"All right. We'll take fifteen men from each crew and start as soon as possible."

Francoise saw Villiers and Harston shoot furtive glances at each other, then lower their gaze quickly as they lifted their wine glasses to hide the murky intent in their eyes. Francoise saw the fatal weakness in Vulmea's plan, and wondered how he could have overlooked it. She knew he would never come out of that forest alive. Once the treasure was in their grasp, the others would form a rogue's alliance long enough to rid themselves of the man both hated. She shuddered, staring morbidly at the man she knew was doomed; strange to see that powerful fighting man sitting there, laughing and swilling wine, in full prime and power, and to know that he was already doomed to a bloody death.

The whole situation was pregnant with bloody portents. Villiers would trick and kill Harston if he could, and she knew that the Englishman had already marked Villiers for death, and doubtless, also, her uncle and herself. If Villiers won the final battle of cruel wits, their lives were safe-but looking at the buccaneer as he sat there chewing his mustache, with all the stark evil of his nature showing naked in his dark face, she could not decide which was more abhorrent --death or Villiers.

"How far is it?" demanded Harston.

"If we start within the hour we can be back before midnight," answered Vulmea.

73

He emptied his glass, rose, hitched at his girdle and looked at Henri.

"D'Chastillon," he said, "are you mad, to kill an Indian hunter'?"

"What do you mean?" demanded Henri, starting.

"You mean to say you don't know that your men killed an Indian in the woods last night?"

"None of my men was in the woods last night," declared the Count.

"Well, somebody was," grunted Vulmea, fumbling in a pocket. "I saw his head nailed to a tree near the edge of the forest. He wasn't painted for war. I didn't find any boot-tracks, from which I judged it'd been nailed up there before the storm. But there were plenty of moccasin tracks on the wet ground. Indians had seen that head. They were men of some other tribe, or they'd have taken it down. If they happen to be at peace with the tribe the dead man belonged to, they'll make tracks to his village and tell his people."

"Perhaps they killed him," suggested Henri.

"No, they didn't. But they know who did, for the same reason that I know. This chain was knotted about the stump of the severed neck. You must have been utterly mad, to identify your handiwork like that."

He drew forth something and tossed it on the table before the Count, who lurched up choking, as his hand flew to his throat. It was the gold seal-chain he habitually wore about his neck.

Vulmea glanced questioningly at the others, and Villiers made a quick gesture to indicate the Count was not quite right in the head. Vulmea sheathed his cutlass and donned his plumed hat.

"All right; let's go."

The captains gulped down their wine and rose, hitching at their sword-belts. Villiers laid a hand on Henri's arm and shook him slightly. The Count started and stared about him, then followed the others out, dazedly, the chain dangling from his fingers. But not all left the hail.

Francoise and Tina, forgotten on the stair as they peeped between the balustrades, saw Gallot loiter behind until the heavy door closed behind the others. Then he hurried to the fireplace and raked carefully at the smoldering coals. He sank to his knees and peered closely at something for along space. Then he rose and stole out of the hall by another door.

"What did he find in the fire?" whispered Tina.

Francoise shook her head, then, obeying the promptings of her curiosity, rose and went down to the empty hall. An instant later she was kneeling where the major domo had knelt, and she saw what he had seen.

It was the charred remnant of the map Vulmea had thrown into the fire. It was ready to crumble at a touch, but faint lines and bits of writing were still discernible upon it. She could not read the writing, but she could trace the outlines of what seemed to be the picture of a hill or crag, surrounded by marks evidently representing dense trees. From Gallot's actions she believed he recognized it as portraying some topographical feature familiar to him. She knew the majordomo had penetrated further inland than any other man of the settlement.

CHAPTER 6

Francoise came down the stair and paused at the sight of Count Henri seated at the table, turning the broken chain about in his hands. The fortress stood strangely quiet in the noonday heat. Voices of people within the stockade sounded subdued, muffled. The same drowsy stillness reigned on the beach outside where the rival crews lay in armed suspicion, separated by a few hundred yards of bare sand. Far out in the bay the War-Hawk lay with a handful of men aboard her, ready to snatch her out of reach at the slightest indication of treachery. The ship was Harston's trump card, his best guarantee against the trickery of his associates.

Vulmea had plotted shrewdly to eliminate the chances of an ambush in the forest by either party, but as far as Francoise could see he had failed utterly to safe-guard himself against the treachery of his companions. He had disappeared into the woods, leading the two captains and their thirty men, and the girl was positive she would never see him alive again.

Presently she spoke, and her voice was strained and harsh.

"When they have the treasure they will kill Vulmea. What then? Are we to go aboard the ship! Can we trust Harston?"

Henri shook his head absently.

"Villiers whispered his plan to me. He will see that night overtakes the treasure-party so they are forced to camp in the forest. He will find a way to kill the Englishmen in their sleep. Then he and his men will come stealthily on to the beach. Just before dawn I will send some of my fishermen secretly from the fort to swim out and seize the ship. Neither Harston nor Vulmea thought of that. Villiers will come out of the forest, and with our united forces we will destroy the pirates camped on the beach. Then we will sail in the War-Hawk with all the treasure."

"And what of me?" she asked with dry lips.

"I have promised you to Villiers," he answered harshly, and without the slightest touch of sympathy. "But for my promise he would not take us off."

He lifted the chain so it caught the gleam of the sun, slanting through a window. "I must have dropped it on the sand," he muttered. "He found it-"

"You did not drop it on the sand," said Francoise, in a voice as devoid of mercy as his own; her soul seemed turned to stone. "You tore it from your throat last night when you flogged Tina. I saw it gleaming on the floor before I left the hall."

He looked up, his face grey with a terrible fear.

She laughed bitterly, sensing the mute question in his dilated eyes.

"Yes! The black man! He was here! He must have found the chain on the floor. I saw him, padding along the upper hallway."

He sank back in his chair, the chain slipping from his nerveless hands.

"In the manor!" he whispered. "In spite of guards and bolted doors! I can no more guard against him than I can escape him! Then it was no dream--that clawing at my door last night! At my door!" he shrieked, tearing at the lace upon his collar as though it strangled him. "God curse him!"

The paroxysm passed, leaving him faint and trembling.

"I understand," he panted, "the bolts on my chamber door balked even him. So he destroyed the ship upon which I might have escaped him, and he slew that wretched savage and left my chain upon him, to bring down the vengeance of his people on me. They have seen that chain upon my neck many a time."

"Who is this black man?" asked Francoise, fear crawling along her spine.

"A juju-man of the Slave Coast," he whispered, staring at her with weird eyes that seemed to look through her and far beyond to some dim doom.

"I built my wealth on human flesh. When I was younger my ships plied between the Slave Coast and the West Indies, supplying black men to the Spanish plantations. My partner was a black wizard of a coasttribe. He captured the slaves with his warriors, and I delivered them to the Indies. I was evil in those days, but he was ten times more evil. If ever a man sold -his soul to the Devil, he was that man. Even now in nightmares I am haunted by the sights I saw in his village when the moon hung red in the jungle trees, and the drums bellowed, and human victims screamed on the altars of his heathen gods.

"In the end I tricked him out of his share of the trade, and sold him to the Spaniards who chained him to a galley's oar. He swore an awful vengeance upon me, but I laughed, for I believed not even he could escape the fate to which I had delivered him.

"As the years passed, however, I could not forget him, and would wake sometimes in fright, his threat ringing in my ears. I told myself that he was dead, long ago, under the lashes of the Spaniards. Then one day there came to me word that a strange black man, with the scars of galley-chains on his wrists, had come to France and was seeking me.

"He knew me by another name, in the old days, but I knew he would trace me out. In haste I sold my lands and put to sea, as you know. With a whole world between us, I thought I would be safe. But he has tracked me down and he is lurking out there, like a coiled cobra."

"What do you mean, 'He destroyed the ship'?' asked Francoise uneasily.

"The wizards of the Slave Coast have the power of raising tempests!" whispered the Count, from grey lips. "Witchcraft!"

Francoise shuddered. That sudden tempest, she knew, had been but a freak of chance; no man could summon a storm at will. And a savage raised in the blackness of a West Coast jungle might be able to enter a fortress guarded by armed men, when there was a mist to blur their sight. This grim stranger was only a man of flesh and blood. But she shivered, remembering a drum that droned exultantly above the whine of the storm-

Henri's weird eyes lit palely as he gazed beyond the tapestried walls to far, invisible horizons.

"I'll trick him yet," he whispered. "Let him delay to strike this night-dawn will find me with a ship under my heels and again I'll cast an ocean between me and his vengeance."

"Hell's fire!"

Vulmea stopped short. Behind him the seamen halted, in two compact clumps. They were following an old Indian path which led due east, and the beach was no longer visible.

"What are you stopping for?" demanded Harston suspiciously.

Somebody's on the trail ahead of us," growled Vulmea. "Somebody in boots. His spoor's not more than an hour old. Did either of you swine send a man ahead of us for any reason?"

Both captains loudly disclaimed any such act, glaring at each other with mutual disbelief. Vulmea shook his head disgustedly and strode on, and the seamen rolled after him. Men of the sea, accustomed to the wide expanses of blue water, they were ill at ease with the green mysterious walls of trees and vines hemming them in. The path wound and twisted until most of them lost all sense of direction.

"Damned peculiar things going on around here," growled Vulmea. "If Henri didn't hang up that Indian's head, who did? They'll believe he did, anyway. That's an insult. When his tribe learns about it, there'll be hell to pay. I hope we're out of these woods before they take the warpath."

When the trail veered northward Vulmea left it, and began threading his way through the dense trees in a southeasterly direction. Harston glanced uneasily at Villiers. This might force a change in their plans. Within a few hundred feet from the path both were hopelessly lost.

Suspicions of many kinds were gnawing both men when they suddenly emerged from the thick woods and saw just ahead of them a gaunt crag that jutted up from the forest floor. A dim path leading out of the woods from the east ran among a cluster of boulders and wound up the crag on a ladder of stony shelves to a flat ledge near the summit.

"That trail is the one I followed, running from the Indians," said Vulmea, halting. "It leads up to a cave behind that ledge. In that cave are the bodies of da Verrazano and his men, and the treasure. But a word before we go up after it: if you kill me here, you'll never find your way back to the trail. I know how helpless you all are in the deep woods. Of course the beach lies due west, but if you have to make your way through the tangled woods, burdened with the plunder, it'll take you days instead of hours. I don't think these woods will be very safe for white men when the Indians learn about that head in the tree."

He laughed at the ghastly, mirthless smiles with which they greeted his recognition of their secret intentions. And he also comprehended the thought that sprang in the mind of each: let the Irishman secure the loot for them, and lead them back to the trail before they killed him.

"Three of us are enough to lug the loot down from the cave," he said.

Harston laughed sardonically.

"Do you think I'm fool enough to go up there alone with you and Villiers? My boatswain comes with me!" He designated a brawny, hard-faced giant, naked to his belt, with gold hoops in his ears, and a crimson scarf knotted about his head.

"And my executioner comes with me!" growled Villiers. He beckoned a lean sea-thief with a face like a parchmentcovered skull, who carried a great scimitar naked over his bony shoulder.

Vulmea shrugged his shoulders. "Very well. Follow me."

They were close on his heels as he strode up the winding path. They crowded him close as he passed through the cleft in the wall behind the ledge, and their breath sucked in greedily as he called their attention to the iron-bound chests on either side of the short tunnel.

"A rich cargo there," he said carelessly. "Garments, weapons, ornaments. But the real treasure lies beyond that door."

He pushed it partly open and drew aside to let his companions look through.

They looked into a wide cavern, lit vaguely by a blue glow that shimmered through it smoky mist-like haze. A great ebon table stood in the midst of the cavern, and in a carved chair with a high back and broad arms sat a giant figure, fabulous and fantastic-there sat Giovanni da Verrazano, his great head sunk on his bosom, one shrivelled hand still gripping a jeweled goblet; da Verrazano. in his plumed hat, his gilt-embroidered coat with jeweled buttons that winked in the blue flame, his flaring boots and gold-worked baldric that upheld a jewel-hilted sword in a golden sheath.

And ranging the board, each with his chin resting on his lace-bedecked breast, sat the eleven buccaneers. The blue fire played weirdly on them, as it played like a nimbus of frozen fire about the heap of curiously-cut gems which shone in the center of the table- the jewels of the Montezumas! The stones whose value was greater than the value of all the rest of the known gems in the world put together!

The faces of the pirates showed pallid in the blue glow.

"Go in and take them," invited Vulmea, and Harston and Villiers crowded past him, jostling one another in their haste. Their followers were treading on their heels. Villiers kicked the door wide open-and halted with one foot on the threshold at the sight of a figure on the floor, previously hidden by the partly-closed door. It was a man, prone and contorted, head drawn back between his shoulders, white face twisted in a grin of mortal agony, clawed fingers gripping his own throat.

"Gallot!" ejaculated Villiers. "What-!" With sudden suspicion he thrust his head into the bluish mist that filled the inner cavern. And he choked and screamed: "There is death in the smoke!"

Even as he screamed, Vulmea hurled his weight against the four men bunched in the doorway, sending them staggering-but not headlong into the cavern as he had planned. They were recoiling at the sight of the dead man and the realization of the trap, and his violent impact, while it threw them off their feet, yet failed of the result he desired. Harston and Villiers sprawled half over the threshold on their knees, the boatswain tumbling over their legs, and the executioner caromed against the wall. Before Vulmea could follow up his intention of kicking the fallen men into the cavern and holding the door against them until the poisonous mist did its deadly work, he had to turn and defend himself against the frothing onslaught of the executioner.

The Frenchman missed a tremendous swipe with his headsman's sword as the Irishman ducked, and the great blade banged against the stone wall, scattering blue sparks. The next instant his skull-faced head rolled on the cavern floor under the bite of Vulmea's cutlass.

In the split seconds this action had consumed, the boatswain regained his feet and fell on the Irishman, raining blows with a cutlass. Blade met blade with a ring of steel that was deafening in the narrow tunnel. The two captains rolled back across the threshold, gagging and purple in the face, too near strangled to shout, and Vulmea redoubled his efforts, striving to dispose of his antagonist so he could cut down his rivals before they could recover from the effects of the poison. The boatswain was driven backward, dripping blood at each step, and he began desperately to bellow for his mates. But before Vulmea could deal the final stroke, the two chiefs, gasping but murderous, came at him with swords in their hands, croaking for their men.

Vulmea bounded back and leaped out onto the ledge, fearing to be trapped by the men coming in response to their captains' yells.

These were not coming as fast as he expected, however. They heard the muffled shouts issuing from the cavern, but no man dared start up the path for fear of a sword in the back. Each band faced the other tensely, grasping weapons but incapable of decision, and when they saw Vulmea bound out on the ledge, they merely gaped. While they stood with their matches smoldering he ran up the ladder of handholds niched in the rock and threw himself prone on the summit of the crag, out of their sight.

The captains stormed out on the ledge and their men, seeing their leaders were not at sword-strokes, ceased menacing each other and gaped in greater bewilderment.

"Dog!" screamed Villiers. "You planned to poison us! Traitor!"

Vulmea mocked them from above.

"What did you expect? You two were planning to cut my throat as soon as I got the plunder for you. If it hadn't been for that fool Gallot I'd have trapped the four of you and explained to your men how you rushed in heedless to your doom!"

"And you'd have taken my ship and all the loot!" frothed Harston.

"Aye! And the pick of both crews! It was Gallot's footprints I saw on the trail. I wonder how the fool learned of this cave."

"If we hadn't seen his body we'd have walked into that death-trap," muttered Villiers, his dark face still ashy. "That blue smoke was like unseen fingers crushing my throat."

"Well, what are you going to do'?" their tormentor yelled sardonically.

"What are we going to do?" asked Villiers of Harston.

"You can't get the jewels," Vulmea assured them with satisfaction from his aerie. "That mist will strangle you. It nearly got me, when I stepped in there. Listen and I'll tell you a tale the Indians tell in their lodges when the fires burn low! Once, long ago, twelve strange men came out of the sea and found a cave and heaped it with gold and gems. But while they sat drinking and singing, the earth shook and smoke came out of the earth and strangled them. Thereafter the tribes all shunned the spot as haunted and accursed by evil spirits.

"When I crawled in there to escape the Indians, I realized that the old legend was true, and referred to da Verrazano. An earthquake must have cracked the rock floor of the cavern they'd fortified, and he and his buccaneers were overcome as they sat at wine by the poisonous fumes of gases welling up from some vent in the earth. Death guards their loot!"

Harston peered into the tunnel mouth.

"The mist is drifting out into the tunnel," he growled, "but it dissipates itself in the open air. Damn Vulmea! Let's climb up after him."

"Do you think any man on earth could climb those handholds against his sword?" snarled Villiers. "We'll have the men up here, and set some to watch and shoot him if he shows himself. He had some plan of getting those jewels, and if he could get them, so can we. We'll tie a hook to a rope, cast it about the leg of that table and drag it, jewels and all, out onto the ledge."

"Well thought, Guillaume!" came down Vulmea's mocking voice. "Just what I had in mind. But how will you find your way back to the path? It'll be dark before you reach the beach, if you have to feel your way through the woods, and I'll follow you and kill you one by one m the dark."

"It's no empty boast," muttered Harston. "He is like an Indian for stealth. If he hunts us back through the forest, few of us will live to see the beach."

"Then we'll kill him here," gritted Villiers. "Some of us will shoot at him while the rest climb the crag. Listen! Why does he laugh?"

"To hear dead men making plots!" came Vulmea's grimly amused voice.

"Heed him not," scowled Villiers, and lifting his voice, he shouted for the men below to join him and Harston on the ledge.

As the sailors started up the slanting trail, there sounded a hum like that of an angry bee, ending in a sharp thud. A buccaneer gasped and sank to his knees, clutching the shaft that quivered in his breast. A yell of alarm went up from his companions.

"What's the matter?" yelled Harston.

"Indians!" bawled a pirate, and went down with an arrow in his neck.

"Take cover, you fools!" shrieked Villiers. From his vantage point he glimpsed painted figures moving in the bushes. One of the men on the winding path fell back dying. The rest scrambled hastily down among the rocks about the foot of the crag. Arrows flickered from the bushes, splintering on the boulders. The men on the ledge lay prone.

"We're trapped!" Harston's face was pale. Bold enough with a deck under his feet, this silent, savage warfare shook his nerves.

"Vulmea said they feared this crag," said Villiers. "When night falls the men must climb up here. The Indians won't rush us on the ledge."

"That's true!" mocked Vulmea. "They won't climb the crag. They'll merely surround it and keep you here until you starve."

"Make a truce with him," muttered Harston. "If any man can get us out of this, he can. Time enough to cut his throat later." Lifting his voice he called: "Vulmea, let's forget our feud. You're in this as much as we are."

"How do you figure that?" retorted the Irishman. "When it's dark I can climb down the other side of this crag and crawl through the line the Indians have thrown around this hill. They'll never see me. I can return to the fort and report you all slain by the savages--which will shortly be the truth!"

Harston and Villiers stared at each other in pallid silence.

"But I'm not going to do that!" Vulmea roared. "Not because I have any love for you dogs, but because a white man doesn't leave white men, even his enemies, to be butchered by red savages."

The Irishman's tousled black head appeared over the crest of the crag.

"Listen! There's only a small band down there. I saw them sneaking through the brush when I laughed, awhile ago. I believe a big war-party is heading in our direction, and those are a group of fleet-footed young braves sent ahead of it to cut us off from the beach.

"They're all on the west side of the crag. I'm going down on the east side and work around behind them. Meanwhile, you crawl down the path and join your men among the rocks. When you hear me yell, rush the trees."

"What of the treasure?"

"To hell with it! We'll be lucky if we get out of here with our scalps."

The black-maned head vanished. They listened for sounds to indicate that Vulmea had crawled to the almost sheer eastern wall and was working his way down, but they heard nothing. Nor did any sound come from the forest. No more arrows broke against the rocks where the sailors were hidden, but all knew that fierce black eyes were watching with murderous patience. Gingerly Harston, Villiers and the boatswain started down the winding path. They were halfway down when the shafts began to whisper around them. The boatswain groaned and toppled down the slope, shot through the heart. Arrows splintered on the wall about the captains as they tumbled in frantic haste down the steep trail. They reached the foot in a scrambling rush and lay panting among the rocks.

"Is this more of Vulmea's trickery?" wondered Villiers profanely.

"We can trust him in this matter," asserted Harston. "There's a racial principle involved here. He'll help us against the Indians, even though he plans to murder us himself. Hark!"

A blood-freezing yell knifed the silence. It came from the woods to the west, and simultaneously an object arched out of the trees, struck the ground and rolled bouncingly toward the rocks-a severed human head, the hideously painted face frozen in a death-snarl.

"Vulmea's signal!" roared Harston, and the desperate pirates rose like a wave from the rocks and rushed headlong toward the woods.

Arrows whirred out of the bushes, but their flight was hurried and erratic. Only three men fell. Then the wild men of the sea plunged through the fringe of foliage and fell on the naked painted figures that rose out of the gloom before them. There was a murderous instant of panting, hand to hand ferocity, cutlasses beating down war-axes, booted feet trampling naked bodies, and then bare feet were rattling through the bushes in headlong flight as the survivors of that brief carnage quit the field, leaving seven still, painted figures stretched on the bloodstained leaves that littered the earth. Further back in the thickets sounded a thrashing and heaving, and then it ceased and Vulmea strode into view, his hat gone, his coat torn, his cutlass dripping in his hand.

"What now?" panted Villiers. He knew the charge had succeeded only because Vulmea's unexpected attack on the rear of the Indians had demoralized the painted men, and prevented them from melting back before the rush.

"Come on!"

They let their dead lie where they had fallen, and crowded close at his heels as he trotted through the trees. Alone they would have sweated and blundered among the thickets for hours before they found the trail that led to the beach-if they had ever found it. Vulmea led them as unerringly as if he had been following an open road, and the rovers shouted with hysterical relief as they burst suddenly upon the trail that ran westward.

"Fool!" Vulmea clapped a hand on the shoulder of a pirate who started to break into a run, and hurled him back among his companions. "You'd burst your heart within a thousand yards. We're miles from the beach. Take an easy gait. We may have to sprint the last mile. Save some of your wind for it. Come on, now."

He set off down the trail at a steady jog-trot, and the seamen followed him, suiting their pace to his.

The sun was touching the waves of the western ocean. Tina stood at the window from which Francoise had watched the storm.

"The sunset turns the ocean to blood," she said. "The ship's sail is a white fleck on the crimson waters. The woods are already darkening."

"What of the seamen on the beach?" asked Francoise languidly. She reclined on a couch, her eyes closed, her hands clasped behind her head.

"Both camps are preparing their supper," answered Tina. "They are gathering driftwood and building fires. I can hear them shouting to one another--what's that?"

The sudden tenseness in the girl's tone brought Francoise upright on her couch. Tina gripped the window sill and her face was white.

"Listen! A howling, far off, like many wolves!"

"Wolves?" Francoise sprang up, fear clutching her heart. "Wolves do not hunt in packs at this time of the year!"

"Look!" shrilled the girl. "Men are running out of the forest!"

In an instant Francoise was beside her, staring wide-eyed at the figures, small in the distance, streaming out of the woods.

"The sailors!" she gasped. "Empty handed! I see Villiers-Harston

"Where is Vulmea?" whispered the girl.

Francoise shook her head.

"Listen! Oh, listen!" whimpered the child, clinging to her.

All in the fort could hear it now--- a vast ululation of mad blood-lust, rising from the depths of the dark forest.

That sound spurred on the panting men reeling toward the stockade.

"They're almost at our heels!" gasped Harston, his face a drawn mask of muscular exhaustion. "My ship--"

"She's too far out for us to reach," panted Villiers. "Make for the fort. See, the men camped on the beach have seen us!" He waved his arms in breathless pantomime, but the men on the strand had already recognized the significance of that wild howling in the forest. They abandoned their fires and cooking-pots and fled for the stockade gate. They were pouring through it as the fugitives from the forest rounded the south angle and reeled into the gate, half dead from exhaustion. The gate was slammed with frenzied haste, and men swarmed up the firing ledge.

Francoise confronted Villiers.

"Where is Black Vulmea?"

The buccaneer jerked a thumb toward the blackening woods. His chest heaved, and sweat poured down his face. "Their scouts were at our heels before we gained the beach. He paused to slay a few and give us time to get away."

He staggered away to take his place on the wall, whither Harston had already mounted. Henri stood there, a somber, cloak-wrapped figure, aloof and silent. He was like a man bewitched.

"Look!" yelped a pirate above the howling of the yet unseen horde.

A man emerged from the forest and raced fleetly toward the fort.

"Vulmea!"

Villiers grinned wolfishly.

"We're safe in the stockade. We know where the treasure is. No reason why we shouldn't put a bullet through him now."

"Wait!" Harston caught his arm. "We'll need his sword! Look!"

Behind the fleeing Irishman a wild horde burst from the forest, howling as they ran-naked savages, hundreds and hundreds of them. Their arrows rained about the fugitive. A few strides more and Vulmea reached the eastern wall of the stockade, bounded high, seized the points of the palisades and heaved himself up and over, his cutlass in his teeth. Arrows thudded venomously into the logs where his body had just been. His resplendent coat was gone, his white silk shirt torn and bloodstained.

"Stop them!" he roared as his feet hit the ground inside. "if they get on the wall we're done for!"

Seamen, soldiers and henchmen responded instantly and a storm of bullets tore into the oncoming horde.

Vulmea saw Francoise, with Tina clinging to her hand, and his language was picturesque.

"Get into the manor," he commanded. "Their arrows will arch over the wall-what did I tell you?" A shaft cut into the earth at Francoise's feet and quivered like a serpent-head. Vulmea caught up a musket and leaped to the firing-ledge. "Some of you dogs prepare torches!" he roared, above the rising clamor of battle. "We can't fight them in the dark!"

The sun had sunk in a welter of blood; out in the bay the men about the ship had cut the anchor chain and the War-Hawk was rapidly receding on the crimson horizon.

CHAPTER 7

Night had fallen, but torches streamed across the strand, casting the mad scene into lurid revealment. Naked men in paint swarmed the beach; like waves they came against the palisade, bared teeth and blazing eyes gleaming in the glare of the torches thrust over the wall.

From up and down the coast the tribes had gathered to rid their country of the white-skinned invaders, and they surged against the stockade, driving a storm of arrows before them, fighting into the hail of bullets and shafts that tore into their masses. Sometimes they came so close to the wall they were hewing at the gate with their war-axes and thrusting their spears through the loopholes. But each time the tide ebbed back, leaving its drift of dead. In this kind of fighting the pirates were at their stoutest. Their matchlocks tore holes in the charging horde, their cutlasses hewed the wild men from the palisades.

Yet again and again the men of the woods returned to the onslaught with all the stubborn ferocity that had been roused in their fierce hearts.

"They are like mad dogs!" gasped Villiers, hacking downward at the savage hands that grasped at the palisade points, the dark faces that snarled up at him.

"If we can hold the fort till dawn they'll lose heart," grunted Vulmea, splitting a feathered skull. "They won't maintain a long siege. Look, they're falling back again."

The charge rolled back and the men on the wall shook the sweat out of their eyes, counted their dead, and took a fresh grasp on the blood-slippery hilts of their swords. Like blood-hungry wolves, grudgingly driven from a cornered prey, the Indians slunk back beyond the ring of torch-light. Only the bodies of the slain lay before the palisades.

"Have they gone?" Harston shook back his wet, tawny locks. The cutlass in his fist was notched and red, his brawny bare arm was splashed with blood.

"They're still out there." Vulmea nodded toward the outer darkness which ringed the circle of torches. He glimpsed movements in the shadows, glitter of eyes and the dull sheen of spears.

"They've drawn off for a bit, though," he said. "Put sentries on the wall and let the rest drink and eat. It's past midnight. We've been fighting steadily for hours."

The captains clambered down, calling their men from the walls. A sentry was posted in the middle of each wall, east, west, north and south, and a clump of soldiers was left at the gate. The Indians, to reach the wall, would have to charge across a wide, torch-lit space, and the defenders could resume their places long before the rush could reach the stockade.

"Where's d'Chastillon?" demanded Vulmea, gnawing a huge beef-bone as he stood beside the fire the men had built in the center of the compound. Englishmen and Frenchmen mingled together, wolfing the meat and wine the women brought them, and allowing their wounds to be bandaged.

"He was fighting on the wall beside me an hour ago," grunted Harston, "when suddenly he stopped short and glared out into the darkness as if he saw a ghost. 'Look!' he croaked. 'The black devil! I see him, out there in the night!' Well, I could swear I saw a strange figure moving among the shadows; it was just a glimpse before it was gone. But Henri jumped down from the wall and staggered into the manor like a man with a mortal wound. I haven't seen him since."

"He probably saw a forest-devil," said Vulmea tranquilly. "The Indians say this coast is lousy with them. What I'm more afraid of is fire-arrows. They're likely to start shooting them at any time. What's that? It sounded like a cry for help!"

When the lull came in the fighting, Francoise and Tina had crept to their window, from which they had been driven by the danger of flying arrows. They watched the men gather about the fire.

"There are not enough sentries on the stockade," said Tina.

In spite of her nausea at the sight of the corpses sprawled about the palisades, Francoise was moved to laugh.

"Do you think you know more about war than the men'?" she chided gently.

"There should be more men on the walls," insisted the child, shivering. "Suppose the black man came back! One man to a side is not enough. The black man could creep beneath the wall and shoot him with a poisoned dart before he could cry out. He is like a shadow, and hard to see by torchlight."

Francoise shuddered at the thought.

"I am afraid," murmured Tina. "I hope Villiers and Harston are killed."

"And not Vulmea?" asked Francoise curiously.

"Black Vulmea would not harm a woman," said the child confidently.

"You are wise beyond your years, Tina," murmured Francoise.

"Look!" Tina stiffened. "The sentry is gone from the south wall! I saw him on the ledge a moment ago. Now he has vanished."

From their window the palisade points of the south wall were just visible over the slanting roofs of a row of huts which paralleled that wall almost its entire length. A sort of open-topped corridor, three or four yards wide, was formed by the stockade-wall and the back of the huts, which were built in a solid row. These huts were occupied by the retainers.

"Where could the sentry have gone?" whispered Tina uneasily.

Francoise was watching one end of the hut-row which was not far from a side door of the manor. She could have sworn she saw a shadowy figure glide from behind the huts and disappear at the door. Was that the vanished sentry? Why had he left the wall, and why should he steal so subtly into the manor? She did not believe it was the sentry she had seen, and a nameless fear congealed her blood.

"Where is the Count, Tina?" she asked.

"In the great hall, my Lady. He sits alone at the table, wrapped in his cloak and drinking wine, with a face grey as death."

"Go and tell him what we have seen. I will keep watch from this window, lest the Indians climb the unguarded wall."

Tina scampered away. Francoise heard her slippered feet pattering along the corridor, receding down the stair. Then suddenly, terribly, there rang out a scream of such poignant fear that Francoise's heart almost stopped with the shock of it. She was out of the chamber and flying down the corridor before she was aware that her limbs were in motion. She ran down the stair-and halted as if turned to stone.

She did not scream as Tina had screamed. She was incapable of sound or motion. She saw Tina, was aware of the reality of small hands grasping frantically. But these

103

were the only realities in a scene of nightmare, and brain-shattering horror.

Out in the stockade Harston had shaken his head at Vulmea's question.

"I heard nothing."

"I did!" Vulmea's wild instincts were roused. "It came from the south wall, behind those huts!"

Drawing his cutlass he strode toward the palisades. From the compound the south wall and the sentry posted there were not visible, being hidden behind the huts. Harston followed, impressed by Vulmea's manner.

At the mouth of the open lane between the huts and the wall Vulmea halted, swearing. The space was dimly lighted by torches flaring at either corner of the stockade. And midway in that natural corridor a crumpled shape sprawled on the ground.

"The sentry!"

"Hawksby!" swore Harston, running forward and dropping on one knee beside the figure. "By Satan, his throat's cut from ear to ear!"

Vulmea swept the alley with a quick glance, finding it empty save for himself, Harston and the dead man. He peered through a loop-hole. No living man moved within the ring of torch-light outside the fort.

"Who could have done this?" he wondered.

"Villiers!" Harston sprang up, spitting fury like a wildcat. "He has set his dogs to stabbing my men in the back! He plans to destroy me by treachery!"

"Wait, Dick!" Vulmea caught his arm. He had glimpsed the tufted end of a dart jutting from the dead pirate's neck. "I don't believe Villiers-"

But the maddened pirate jerked away and rushed around the end of the but row, breathing blasphemies. Vulmea ran after him, swearing. Harston made straight toward the fire by which Villiers' tall form was visible as the buccaneer chief quaffed a jack of ale.

His amazement was supreme when the jack was dashed violently from his hand, spattering his breastplate with foam, and he was jerked around to confront the convulsed face of the Englishman.

"You murdering dog!" roared Harston. "Will you slay my men behind my back while they fight for your filthy hide as well as for mine'?"

On all sides men ceased eating and drinking to gape in amazement.

"What do you mean?" sputtered Villiers.

"You've set your men to murdering mine at their posts!" bellowed Harston.

"You lie!" Smoldering hate burst into sudden flame.

With a howl Harston heaved up his cutlass and cut at the Frenchman's head. Villiers caught the blow on his armored left arm and sparks flew as he staggered back, ripping out his own sword.

In an instant the captains were fighting like madmen, their blades flaming and flashing in the firelight. Their crews reacted instantly and blindly. A deep roar went up as Englishmen and Frenchmen drew their swords and fell upon one another. The pirates left on the walls abandoned their posts and leaped down into the stockade, blades in hand. In an instant the compound was swarming with battling groups of men. The soldiers at the gate turned and stared down in amazement, forgetful of the enemy lurking outside.

It had all happened so quickly ---smoldering passions exploding into sudden battle- that men were fighting all over the compound before Vulmea could reach the maddened captains. Ignoring the swords that flashed about his ears, he tore them apart with such violence that they staggered backward and Villiers tripped and fell headlong.

"You cursed fools, will you throw away all our lives?"

Harston was frothing, and Villiers was bawling for assistance. A buccaneer ran at Vulmea and cut at him from behind. The Irishman half turned and caught his arm, checking the stroke in midair.

"Look, you fools!" he roared, pointing with his sword.

Something in his tone caught the attention of the battle-crazed mob. Men froze in their places, with lifted swords, and twisted their heads to stare. Vulmea was pointing at a soldier on the wall. The man was reeling, clawing the air, choking as he tried to shout. Suddenly he pitched to the ground and all saw the shaft standing up between his shoulders.

A yell of alarm rose from the compound. On the heels of the shout came a clamor of blood-freezing screams, the shattering impact of axes on the gate. Flaming arrows arched over the wall and stuck in logs, and thin wisps of blue smoke curled upward. Then from behind the huts along the south wall dark figures came gliding.

"The Indians are in!" roared Vulmea.

Bedlam followed his yell. The freebooters ceased their feud, some turned to meet the savages already within the stockade, some to spring to the wall. The painted men were pouring from behind the huts and their axes clashed against the cutlasses of the sailors.

Villiers was struggling to his feet when a painted savage rushed upon him from behind and brained him with a waraxe.

Vulmea led the Frenchmen against the Indians inside the stockade, and Harston, with most of his men, climbed on the firing-ledge, slashing at the dark figures already swarming up on the wall. The savages, who had crept up unobserved while the defenders of the fort were fighting among themselves, were attacking from all sides. Henri's soldiers were clustered at the gate, trying to hold it against a howling swarm of blood-mad demons.

More and more savages scaled the undefended south wall and streamed from behind the huts. Harston and his men were beaten back from the north and west walls and in an instant the compound was swarming with naked warriors who came over the palisades in a wave. They dragged down the defenders like wolves dragging down a stag; the battle resolved into swirling whirlpools of painted figures surging about small clumps of desperate white men. Bloodsmeared braves dived into the huts and the shrieks that rose as women and children died beneath the red axes rose above the roar of the battle. The soldiers abandoned the gate when they heard those cries, and in an instant the savages had burst it in and were pouring into the stockade at that point also. Huts began to go up in flames.

"Make for the manor!" roared Vulmea, and a dozen men surged in behind him as he hewed a red way through the snarling pack.

Harston was at his side, wielding his red cutlass like a cleaver.

"We can't hold the manor," grunted the Englishman.

"Why not'?" Vulmea was too busy with his crimson work to spare a glance.

"Because-uh!" A knife in a savage hand sank deep in the pirate's back. "Devil eat you, dog!" Harston turned and split the savage's head, then reeled and fell to his knees, blood starting from his lips.

"The manor's burning!" he croaked, and slumped over in the dust.

Vulmea glared about him. The men who had followed him were all down in their blood. An Indian gasping out his life under his feet was the last of the group which had barred his way. All about him battle swirled and surged, but for the moment he stood alone. A few strides and he could leap to the wall, swing over and be gone through the night. But he remembered the helpless girls in the manor-from which, now, smoke was rolling in billowing masses. He ran toward the manor.

A feathered chief wheeled from the door, lifting a war-axe, and behind the Irishman groups of fleet-footed braves were converging upon him. He did not check his stride. His downward sweeping cutlass met and deflected the axe and crushed the skull of the wielder, and an instant later he was through the door and had slammed and bolted it against the axes that splintered into the wood.

The great hall was full of drifting wisps of smoke through which he groped, half blinded. Somewhere a woman was sobbing hysterically. He emerged from a whorl of smoke and stopped dead in his tracks.

The hall was dim and shadowy with the drifting smoke; the silver candelabrum was overturned, the candles extinguished. The only illumination was a lurid glow from the great fireplace and the flames which licked from burning floor to smoking roof beams. And against that lurid glare Vulmea saw a human form swinging slowly at the end of a rope. The dead face turned toward him as the body swung, and it was distorted beyond recognition. But Vulmea knew it was Count Henri d'Chastillon, hanging from his own roof beam.

He saw Francoise and Tina, clutched in each others' arms, crouching at the foot of the stair. And he saw something else, dimly through the smoke--a giant black man, looming against the red glare like a black devil stalking out of hell. The scarred, twisted face, dim in the smoke, was fiendish, the eyes burned red as the reflection of flame on black waters. At the stark evil of that face even the fierce pirate felt a chill along his spine. And then the shadow of death fell across him as he saw the long bamboo tube in the black man's hand.

Slowly, gloatingly the black man lifted it to his lips, and Vulmea knew winged death would strike him before he could reach the killer with his sword. His desperate eyes fell on a massive silver bench, ornately carven, once part of the splendor of Chateau d'Chastillon. It stood at his feet. With desperate quickness he grasped it and heaved it above his head.

"Take this to hell with you!" he roared in a voice like a clap of wind, and hurled the bench with all the power of his iron muscles, even as the dart leaped from the lifted bamboo. In midair it splintered on the hurtling bench, and full on the broad black breast crashed a hundred pounds of silver. The impact shattered bones and carried the black man off his feet-hurled him backward into the open fireplace. A horrible scream shook the hall. The mantel cracked and stones fell from the great chimney, half hiding the black, writhing limbs. Burning beams crashed down from the roof and thundered on the stones, and the whole heap was enveloped by a roaring burst of flames.

'Fire was licking at the stair when Vulmea reached it. He caught up Tina under one arm and dragged Francoise to her feet. Through the crackle and snap of the flames sounded the splintering of the door under the war-axes.

He glared about, sighted a door at the other end of the hall, and hurried through it, half carrying, half dragging his dazed charges. As they came into the chamber beyond, a reverberation behind them told them that the roof was falling in the hall. Through a strangling cloud of smoke Vulmea saw an open, outer door on the other side of the chamber. As he lugged his charges through it, he saw that the lock had been forced.

"The black man came in by this door!" Francoise sobbed hysterically. "I saw him-but I did not know--"

They emerged into the fire-lit compound, a few yards from the hut-row that lined the south wall. A warrior was skulking toward the door, eyes red in the firelight, axe lifted. Turning the girl on his arm away from the blow, Vulmea drove his cutlass through the Indian's breast, and ran toward the south wail.

The enclosure was full of smoke clouds that hid half the red work going on there, but the fugitives had been seen. Naked figures, black against the red glare, pranced out of the smoke, brandishing axes. They were only a few yards behind him when Vulmea ducked into the space between the huts and the wall. At the other end of the lane he saw other warriors running to cut him off. He tossed Francoise bodily to the firing-ledge and leaped after her. Swinging her over the palisades he dropped her to the sand outside and dropped Tina after her. A thrown axe crashed into a log by his shoulder, and then he too was over the wall and gathering up his helpless charges. When the Indians reached the wall the space before the palisades was empty of any living humans.

Dawn was tinging the dim waters with an old rose hue. Far out across the tinted waters a fleck of white grew out of the mist-a sail that seemed to hang suspended in the pearly sky. On a bushy headland Black Vulmea held a ragged cloak over a fire of green wood. As he manipulated the cloak, puffs of smoke rose upward.

Francoise sat near him, one arm about Tina.

"Do you think they'll see it and understand?"

"They'll see it, right enough," he assured her. "They've been hanging off and on this coast all night, hoping to sight some survivors. They're scared stiff. There's only a dozen of them, and not one can navigate well enough to reach the Horn, much less round it. They'll understand my signal; it's a trick the lads of the Brotherhood learned from the Indians. They know I can navigate, and they'll be glad enough to pick us up. Aye, and to give me command of the ship. I'm the only captain left."

"But suppose the Indians see the smoke?" She shuddered, glancing back over the misty sands and bushes to where, miles to the north, a column of smoke stood up in the still air.

"Not likely. After I hid you in the woods last night I sneaked back and saw them dragging barrels of wine out of the storehouses. Most of them were reeling already. They'll be lying around dog-drunk by this time. If I had a hundred men I could wipe out the whole horde. Look! The War-Hawk's coming around and heading for the shore. They've seen the signal."

He stamped out the fire and handed the cloak back to Francoise, who watched him in wonder. The night of fire and blood, and the flight through the black woods afterward, had not shaken his nerves. His tranquil manner was genuine. Francoise did not fear him; she felt safer with him than she had felt since she landed on that wild coast. The man had his own code of honor, and it was not to be despised.

"Who was that black man?" he asked suddenly.

She shivered "A man the Count sold as a galley-slave long ago. Somehow he escaped and tracked us down. My uncle believed him to be a wizard."

"He might have been," muttered Vulmea. "I've seen some queer things on the Slave Coast. But no matter. We have other things to think of. What will you do when you get back to France?"

She shook her head helplessly. "I do not know. I have neither money nor friends. Perhaps it would have been better had one of those arrows struck my heart."

"Do not say that, my Lady!" begged Tina. "I will work for us both!"

Vulmea drew a small leather bag from inside his girdle.

"I didn't get Montezuma's jewels," he rumbled, "but here are some baubles I found in the chest where I got these clothes." He spilled a handful of flaming rubies into his palm. "They're worth a fortune, themselves."

He dumped them back into the bag and handed it to her.

"But I can't take these-" she began.

"Of course you'll take them! I might as well leave you for the Indians to scalp as to take you back to France to starve."

"But what of you?"

Vulmea grinned and nodded toward the swiftly approaching War-Hawk.

"A ship and a crew are all I want. As soon as I set foot on that deck I'll have a ship, and as soon as I raise the coast of Darien I'll have a crew. I'll take a galley and free its slaves, or raid some Spanish plantation on the coast. There are plenty of stout French and British lads toiling as slaves to the Dons, and waiting the chance to escape and join some captain of the Brotherhood. And, as soon as I get back on the Main, and put you and the girl on some honest ship bound for France, I'll show the Spaniards that Black Vulmea still lives! Nay, nay, no thanks! What are a handful of gems to me, when all the loot of the western world is waiting for me!"